THE GLOB WHO GIRDLED GRANVILLE
and
THE SECRET LIVES OF ACTORS

Other Books by Peter Grandbois

The Gravedigger
The Arsenic Lobster: A Hybrid Memoir
Nahoonkara
Domestic Disturbances

Wordcraft Series of Fabulist Novellas

Wait Your Turn/The Stability of Large Systems

NUMBER 2 — WORDCRAFT SERIES OF FABULIST NOVELLAS

PETER GRANDBOIS

A DOUBLE MONSTER FEATURE

THE GLOB WHO GIRDLED GRANVILLE

AND

THE SECRET LIVES OF ACTORS

WORDCRAFT OF OREGON, LLC

La Grande, OR • 2014

Acknowledgments

Thank you to Mike Croley, Jane Delury, and Margot Singer for their sharp editorial eyes.

Thanks, also, to David Memmott for his vision and commitment to all things monstrous.

Finally, thank you to my wife, Tanya, for putting up with the monster in me.

ISBN: 978-1-877655-84-5
Library of Congress Number: 2014942463

Number Two in the Wordcraft Series of Fabulist Novellas

First Edition
October 2014

Cover Design: Kristin Summers, www.redbatdesign.com
Author photo: Gary Isaacs

Published by
Wordcraft of Oregon, LLC
PO Box 3235
La Grande, OR 97850
http://www.wordcraftoforegon.com
info@wordcraftoforegon.com

Member of Council of Literary Magazines & Presses (CLMP)

Text set in Garamond Premier Pro
Printed in United States

THE GLOB WHO GIRDLED GRANVILLE

"Oh, this is the animal that never was..."
—Rilke

GRANVILLE, OHIO is not generally known for its human oddities, and yet it doesn't take more than a casual perusal of the archives of the town paper to immerse oneself in a vast sea of the grotesque, a veritable carnival of mad clowns, monkey-faced boys, and mermaid girls who've lost their way. We read about them and feel inside this could never happen to us. We would never do such a thing. And yet there they are, day after day, year after year, in the annals of this small-town paper. People like you and me who've reached a crossroads, people who make choices, people who cannot bear to keep the monster inside any more. We look at them and say there but for the grace of God go I. It is a lack of imagination on our part. Nothing more. How else can we explain the article from October 4th, 1972 regarding one Gregory Glob of 116 Joy Lane?

The story, if we are to trust it, records how Gregory walked out of his Dutch Colonial house, stood on the doorstep and split in two. He later swore he didn't know why he did it. In fact, he said he wasn't aware of the split at all for most of the first week. But what would Mrs. Glob have said, had she been interviewed? Would she have mentioned the haunting peculiarity of his hesitation in the doorway? She would most certainly recall how he kissed her on the cheek, leaving only the usual slime. But would she remember how he stopped and looked back at her before stepping onto the porch? Would she remember the frightening beauty of his smile, the way it seemed to sense what was to come? It is unfortunate we don't have a photograph from the scene to aid us in our story.

Let us now imagine Gregory bidding adieu to his wife. He kisses her. He thinks to himself that he may not come home directly after work. In fact, he might have a beer with a friend. He has no suspicion of what is before him. No understanding of the ways in which the body acts out when the mind falls prey to its own traps and labyrinths. If he is aware of anything at all, it is of a feeling in his gut akin to hunger. A churning. A gnawing inside just painful enough to lie on the edge of consciousness. He shuffles toward the door and stops. To say he turns to look at his wife might be too strong. It's difficult to spot eyes and mouth in a gelatinous mass. Yet, we understand what Mrs. Glob must have been feeling when she saw her husband in the doorway, the morning sun coloring his body deep red. We feel the unstated fear, her own intuition that he might not be coming home, at least not the glob he'd been. We see in her eyes the longing to hang onto the husband that was, the husband who is already gone, even as he now stands in the doorway. If we could locate his mouth as she must be able to—how else do they kiss?—then we, too, would see that strange smile, we, too, would feel the apprehension only a spouse can feel that her life may be irrevocably altered without her knowledge and with no way to control the outcome. If we could but look through her eyes, we might see the glob for what he's been these past months. Imagine for a moment that we'd been there, that we'd seen the tell

8

tale signs of despair, the way in which our glob slowly, almost imperceptibly began leaving earlier for work in the mornings, eating only toast instead of his normal cereal and toast, kissing his wife on the cheek instead of the lips, often forgetting to say goodbye to his children completely, how he tended to isolate himself at work, to stay in his cubicle, staring at the same sentence on his computer over and over, how when he came home he often went straight to the bedroom feigning a headache rather than greet his wife, and how ever so slowly he'd begun to take a whiskey before bed, first just a sip, but then filling the glass nearly to the top. All the signs were there for even the casual observer to see.

Let us stand clear now and let the troubling story unfold, as we know it did from the newspaper accounts that came after. Of course, we don't have all the details. We don't need them. We know in our hearts what happened, what had to happen given the circumstances. Watch now as the door shuts and Gregory's gelatinous body begins to shake. At first, he appears sad, but as we open further, as we let ourselves be carried into the story, we find his quivering mass disarming. To see an adult shake like that, the way a child shakes when it cries. We want to believe he's shivering because of the cold, though we know better. It's a brisk morning but nothing out of the ordinary, especially for early autumn. The shivering turns to a violent shaking, and we wonder if this is what birth was like for poor Gregory. Of course, even with our strong storyteller's sense of empathy, we'll never fully understand the mysterious life cycle of such a creature. All we really know is that he arrived here on a meteor, a mere babe of an amoeba fourteen short years before. His first experience of life one of hostility as that old man who discovered him poked him with a stick. That stick—and the old man—became Gregory's first meal. Those early days were difficult for Gregory to overcome, both emotionally and legally. This much we do know, as it's a matter of public record. After the old man, he managed to eat quite a few people, including: Dr. Hallen and his nurse, a mechanic, a grocery store janitor, even a bar full of late night drinkers, not to mention those people who never made it out of the Colonial Movie Theatre. And that was all before he reached adolescence! The only thing that saved him from a life in prison—What prison could keep him, really?—was the fact that he'd been so young when he committed the crimes. His lawyers said he was lucky, and he'd probably thought so himself until this day. After a brief three-year sentence in the Arctic Circle, they let him out on good behavior. Maybe that's why he shivers. He never did like the cold, and now any hint of it probably reminds him of that terrible time as an adolescent on the ice. Can you imagine the loneliness, the despair? It would have done any of us in, and would have been the end of Gregory if it hadn't been for Mrs. Glob, aka Jane Martin, the girl he trapped with Steve McQueen in the basement of the diner during his murderous rampage. The threat of asphyxiation down in that basement, the glob seeping in through the cracks all around her, had turned her on. She couldn't possibly stay with Steve after that. Gregory received her first love letter two months into his sentence. Two years later, they were married by correspondence.

The separation begins at the top of his body. We might guess it begins with his head, but it would be exactly that, a mere guess since we're not sure where his head is. The shaking continues, rocking him violently up and down, back and forth, and doesn't stop until he has completely split in two. Then both Gregorys—if we can call them that—rest for a moment on the doorstep, breathing deeply, their entire bodies rising and falling with each breath, until suddenly one of them (let us call him Gregory One) oozes down the steps and into his car, and the other (Gregory Two) heads down the suburban sidewalk toward a rare Friday morning open house—a three-bedroom Cape Cod style only two doors down.

We are left in a bit of a predicament. Who do we imagine we follow? Which glob is the real Gregory? Are they both real? Can half of someone still be that same someone? We must hurry and decide before both, or either, fade from our mind. If only we could split in the same way. To live life as two people, what we wouldn't give for that chance. Why stop at two? What if we could be three, four, or an infinite number? We'd never have to worry about choices like these, choices that keep us up late into the night, choices that paralyze us. Gregory One took the car, probably to work. But we can't be sure. It would be vain searching for him. We can follow him later. Gregory Two entered the open house two doors down from his own. That much is substantiated by the police report. We know where he is, even if we're not sure who he is. Let us hurry.

What we imagine we see through the window is not a pretty picture, the realtor running about the living room, screaming, with Gregory Two sliming all over him, until finally Gregory dissolves the realtor's skin, sinew, and bone. He pulsates on the Berber carpet, sucking up the last bits, growing larger until he is close to the size he was before the split. We hope this relapse isn't indicative of things to come. He'd led such an exemplary life since his rehabilitation. Unfortunately, we have the record as our guide. Still, we hope there are some take away lessons here. Why else go through the trouble of imagining this story?

Gregory Two contracts and expands, in and out, over and over, as if practicing his own form of yoga. We can't help but wonder if he is somehow preparing himself, gathering his strength for what is to come. Perhaps he is simply afraid. The truth is, how many of us would have the courage to walk out on our lives like that? How many of us, even if we could split down the center like Gregory, would dare to start life anew? Think carefully. It's easy to daydream about a different life, even speaking the words holds a certain magic, but to actually do it, to actually sever ourselves from all that we know, all that defines who we are. That takes either courage or foolishness. Which of the two guides our glob remains to be seen.

At last, he gathers himself from the carpet and slides over to the fireplace. He peruses the books lining the mantle before selecting one, then flicks the switch to the gas and settles into the La-Z-Boy recliner in front of the fire. He opens the book, *The Tales and Sketches* of Nathaniel Hawthorne and reads the morning away. It is not until he has finished "Roger Malvin's Burial" and made it halfway through "Wakefield" that he realizes he has stopped shaking. In fact, he is breathing easier than he has done in a long time. He would have to go back to deep childhood in the meteor, hurtling through space on his way to earth to find a time when he felt more relaxed, more like himself. He thinks he could get used to this new life, though he is still not sure exactly what this new life is, only that he is suddenly aware that his wife is not throwing him the evil eye because he is reading. She is not demanding he scratch another item off the "To-Do" list or, worse yet, spend time with her. He thinks, too, how quiet it seems without his two children, Henry and Elizabeth (named after Jane's parents), shouting "Daddy!" every five minutes, as in: "Daddy, I need help with homework!" or "Daddy! Henry hit me again!" or "Daddy, Elizabeth won't play with me!" He closes his eyes, sinks back in the chair and realizes that not even the dog, Davey, can bother him with his incessant chasing of the ghost mouse. Two years before, Davey had caught a mouse beside the bookshelf in the living room and ever since he prowls that bookshelf, barking, reliving his one heroic exploit any time the children raise the noise level or even when it suddenly gets quiet. Any change in his normal routine sets him to barking.

Look at Gregory now, falling asleep in the La-Z-Boy, the book riding his chest. We must make note of this and note, too, the fact that we feel nervous for him, as if we don't quite believe or don't want to believe his state of relaxation will last. It is frightening to observe others successfully achieving what you most desire.

He wakes the next morning, and, instead of his normal routine of cereal and toast for breakfast, he immediately picks up the folk guitar leaning decoratively on a stand in the den. He's never played guitar before. We're not even sure he's ever wanted to. Yet, this lack of previous desire or ability doesn't stop him. It's difficult to describe how he holds the guitar, being a glob. It is quite probably our greatest imaginative act, and we're not sure we're up to it. Still we try. We see how one tentacle forms on his left side, oozing about the neck of the guitar just as another tentacle forms on his right. Being a glob, he can even turn his right hand into a pick. He'll save money on that in the long run.

He strums. Not a pretty sound. Not at all. Most people would put the guitar back at this point, but not our glob. He reconfigures the finger-like appendages he's shaped on his left hand and tries again. A little better. He puts the guitar down, and we must admit we're relieved. Thank God, he's not going to push it. Maybe now he'll go back to reading or mow the lawn, do something sensible. But instead he scours the den, looking for what we're not sure. He checks the bookshelves, then turns to the desk and rifles through the drawers. Nothing. He appears to be giving up, but at the last moment opens the credenza and removes the old tax returns. There at the bottom of the cabinet he finds *Mel Bay's Basic Guitar Vol. 1*. He smiles, sits back in his chair, and opens the book. How dare he do this! How dare he break away and live the life he desires when we can only sit here in our writing chair and imagine the lives of others. We're finished filling in the cracks of his sordid story! Leave him to his own devices. We know how this turns out anyway, and it's not pretty!

He plays a D chord. He actually strums a D, and though we hate to admit it, it sounds pretty good. Then he starts singing *Down in the Valley*. We used to sing that song at camp so many years ago. We loved that song. That time was so full of possibility. We tried archery, canoeing, rock climbing. We even joined the others skinny-dipping on the last night. That was a different time. A time before we became afraid. A time before we had to live our lives through others. Just see how the smile curls about his mouth. How he's tapping his foot to the rhythm. It's here we must say how much we like our job. Yes, we know we were nervous in the previous paragraph but just look! We are bearing witness to a fellow creature discovering himself, even if he is not yet aware of what he's doing. He's on the verge of a Herculean act, an act so great we can feel it working its way through our own flesh and blood. With any luck, one day we will be capable of such an act ourselves. We hope it's not premature to say, "Thank you, Gregory!"

The first week passed much like the first day. Gregory Two practiced feverishly all day then read in the evening until he fell asleep in the La-Z-Boy. Each night just as he drifted to sleep he thought how he'd never been happier. Sure, occasionally Elizabeth or Henry's cherubic face would appear for a brief instant in his dreams, but usually they were shouting for him, and in the dreams he simply picked up Hawthorne's weighty *Tales and Sketches*, turned the page, and their faces disappeared. Of his poor wife, he rarely thought at all, not even in his dreams.

Very little else of import happened, with the exception of the fact that another unfortunate realtor appeared at the front door a week after Gregory had eaten the first. He'd sworn he wouldn't eat anyone else. He'd told himself that murder was part of his old life. Killing people had no place in the life of the folk singer he hoped to become. Yet, within a minute after he invited the realtor in, he pounced on the poor soul. He told himself later that he'd had to do it, the realtor was asking too many questions.

Immediately after eating the second realtor, without stopping to consider what he was doing, Gregory Two dressed in his old clothes—the ones he'd worn on his arrival in his new home—and walked back down the street toward his old house. Had he forgotten why he'd left in the first place? Was it some form of amnesia? Had he seen Gregory One leaving for work five minutes earlier, it might have shocked him from his stupor, but instead, he marched up the porch steps and opened the door. *Don't do it, Gregory! We want to shout. Don't throw away the work you've done. Think of the pain it will cause, not the least of all to us!*

It is only the shuffling sound of his own (shall we say) "foot" stepping across the threshold that wakes him at the critical moment. He stands in the doorway as he'd done that morning one week earlier, trying to figure out what has brought him to this point. Habit, dear Gregory Two, is hard to break. We are bound by routines we cannot fathom. Think yourself lucky that your wife is currently in the laundry and so cannot hear the door opening, cannot hear your panicked breath. Or, perhaps, luck has nothing to do with it. We should be more careful in assigning too great a role to providence in our lives, especially when we foolishly imply that same providence is taking sides, choosing one life over the other. Let us say, simply, that Gregory Two was given a second chance, though even that implies the hand of fate at work. Whatever the case, we are grateful that he seems to have forgotten his reason for coming and heads quickly back to his new home, passing the neighbor, Mrs. Fielding, on the sidewalk. He nods his head to her and mumbles a good morning, but

16

she looks at him as if she's never seen him before. He shuffles on without thinking about it until he hits his yard, then turns around and observes Mrs. Fielding. The same blue jacket as every morning covers the scoliosis that continues to bend her back with each passing year. The same shock of white hair. It was her, wasn't it? Why did she give him that look? He runs now to his new house, locks the door behind him, and peers out the window at his old house. It looks the same, doesn't it? No. There is something different about the aluminum siding. The color is not as white as it once was. Is that it? The pitch of the roof not quite as steep. He's not sure. Did they have a two-car garage or one? He closes his eyes, tries to picture his old house in his mind, but can't. The one he's just seen mixes itself with his vision.

He searches the master closet, finds clothes that will fit him, a hat and glasses that will disguise his head. He studies himself in the bathroom mirror. Not good enough. He rummages through a drawer and finds makeup left by the previous occupants. He applies a base that turns his normally red skin orange. He pencils in eyebrows and even a mustache. It is done. He is another man. He looks again in the mirror and doesn't even recognize himself. Ah, foolish Gregory Two! He doesn't understand that he has already changed. There is no need for a disguise. He is not the man he once was. Why does he suppose Mrs. Fielding didn't recognize him? Our Gregory still believes he has control over who he is, that he is the history of his habits. He confuses habit with identity. Who we are runs much deeper than that, dear Gregory! The rate and constancy of the body's metamorphosis far outpaces any superficial appearance, any cursory behaviors or personality. Like a flower imagining sun and snow, the daily opening and closing of that which lives in the body would leave us breathless if we could truly perceive it. But then again these are mere words. Beautiful words, we might add. We are more skilled at writing than we'd imagined. And yet, if we are honest, upon rereading these words, we wonder if we understand them ourselves. Yes, we can see what they mean, but do we comprehend them the way the body of a child comprehends the passing of joy? We read them and reread them and fear we know their value all too well.

Gregory Two gathers his courage and steps outside, moving toward his former life, though if we asked him he would not be able to tell us why. He passes Mrs. Fielding's house and hesitates. Should he go on? It is only one more house, he tells himself. It is not that far. Fool! It is another world. You have no idea of the shock in store for you. The dead have more chance of re-visiting their homes! Oh, what we wouldn't give to help him avoid this fate. That first week showed such promise. Gregory Two, please, for all our sakes turn around!

Taking a deep breath, he shambles on, slowly moving up the path to the front porch, nervously looking about for fear of being noticed. Two cardinals chase each other through the trees. A black-capped chickadee whistles its *fee-bee, chickadee-dee*, as if this morning is no different from any other. It is then our glob spots his wife through the window, kissing their children on the forehead, then helping them on with their backpacks for school.

When his children make their way to the front door, he panics and hides behind the azaleas. They leave the house, wave goodbye to their mother, then walk down the street, each lost in his own little world: Henry playacting being shot by a machine gun, then a tank, then blown up by a grenade, as he does every morning; Elizabeth reading as she walks, a different book each day. Today it's *The Witch of Blackbird Pond*. Davey runs after them to the limit of the white picket fence, then barks, begging them to take him with them. Not a word about poor Gregory Two. But then why should they miss him? Nothing has changed in their world. Gregory One still tucks them in bed at night, still wakes them in the morning. Their routine remains the same. Only his world has shifted. Surely, the children must have noticed the fact that their father's mass had been reduced. But then again globs put on weight so easily. Gregory One was probably already back to normal. Still, the children must sense the spirit gone from their father, the way he apathetically mopes around the house. No. That's exactly what he'd been like before the split. Despite the evidence, Gregory Two is slow to realize his own children know nothing of what has happened to him.

He moves to the front door. Does he dare to open it, to enter his old life? Would that we had an entire novel instead of these few, paltry pages to explore the ways in which an influence beyond our control pushes every action, each decision we think we make. He pulls the door open and oozes inside, only to become paralyzed with fear in the entry. He hears his wife scrubbing the stovetop. That seems normal enough, though he can't be sure as he used to be at work each day at this time. He looks about the house. The kitchen lies around the corner to his left. Stairs directly in front of him lead to the upper level bedrooms. The living room immediately to his right. Henry's toy guns and Legos litter the floor. Dirty socks hang over the brown leather couch and loveseat. Elizabeth's sandals sit atop the fish tank, where she puts them so the dog won't eat them. Nothing out of the norm. And yet, it doesn't feel right. Not right at all.

He studies the fish tank, which is not the same fish tank, though it must be the same fish tank. He counts the fish. Fourteen. They are the same fish, he thinks, though he's never completely sure, as they die so fast, and the children want them replaced with new ones. The plants. Their color is duller, that's it. It's faded to blue. Or maybe not. Maybe the water is simply dirty, the chemical balance off.

His wife sings to herself. *I'd want no others, if you'd grant me just one more chance.* He's heard this tune before, he's sure of it. Nearly sure. It's Sinatra. No, Bing Crosby, isn't it? He recognizes it now, though he never thought Jane liked the old crooners, and he certainly didn't realize she sang them when she was alone. *Still I'm hoping all the while, you'll give me just one more word.* The more she sings, the more panic overruns him. His chest constricts. His mind goes blank. His eyes (if we can call them that) have trouble focusing. *But now I'm back to cry my heart out for just one more chance.* It's as if the house is shifting keys. He cannot hear himself think. Cannot feel himself in it. *We spend our lives groping for happiness. I found it once and tossed it aside.* He scrambles for the door but the door is no longer where he thought it was, and he runs into the wall. *I've paid for it with hours of loneliness. I've nothing to hide. I'd bury my pride for... buh, buh, buh, bum...* He gropes wildly for the way out and knocks a vase from an alcove in the entry.

"Who's there?" his wife shouts. "Is someone at the door?" She hurries to the entry, broomstick held aloft like a weapon.

Gregory Two has only enough time to make sure his glasses and hat are still in place before his wife enters. "Who are you and what are you doing in my house?" she shouts, though she is only a few feet from him. He's never seen her like this before. Suspicious. Protective. She looks as if she is capable of anything.

"I'm sorry, ma'am," he begins. "I was just passing by, and the door was open." He fumbles with his glasses, almost knocks them off his face. "Your singing. It was . . . beautiful. I don't know what came over me. Before I knew it, I'd stepped inside."

"And knocked over my vase."

"Yes. I'm terribly sorry." He bends to pick up the pieces just as she also bends to clean up, and they bump heads, or at least what we assume is his head. Anatomy is just so difficult to get right, especially when describing creatures whose body continually morphs to fit any available space.

"That was silly of me," she says, laughing.

"It was my fault," he replies. "I'm so clumsy." He is smiling, we are almost sure of it. We can tell by the way her eyes widen, how she responds with a slight tilt of her head, how she reaches out to touch him, to assure him that it's okay, and, perhaps, to assure him of something else. Be careful, Gregory Two! Of such seemingly innocent beginnings do we weave our ends. Do not heed her siren's call! If we had wax, and if we could determine where your ears were, we would stuff those ears to save you. Remember the peace you felt as you sat in that La-

Z-Boy, the sense of freedom that coursed through your veins as you plucked the guitar. You've inspired us with your actions. Some of us actually signed up for piano lessons yesterday, one even ventured toward the oboe!

For some strange reason, the encounter makes him feel warm inside. The best kind of feeling for a glob. Yes, it seems pleasant enough. Yet, we can't help but feel he is heading into the unknown, into a dangerous country from which he will not escape. He reaches out a hand, or should we say a mass of goo seems to extend from his body. "My name is Dr. Hallen, Dr. Thomas Hallen." As soon as the words are out of his mouth, he regrets it. How stupid could he be! It was the first name to come to mind. The third person he'd ever eaten. The old man didn't even have a name, at least he'd never caught it. She'll see him for a fraud now for sure. He breaks out in a cold sweat, or, perhaps, it's simply slime. His smile transforms into a monstrous grimace. He's got to get out as soon as possible. "I'm sorry," he stammers. "I have a patient to see." And he turns and shuffles quickly down the sidewalk.

"Have we met before, Dr. Hallen?" his wife calls out after him, waving goodbye, as she does so. "Your face is so familiar." In answer, Gregory Two increases his pace.

We must ask ourselves what this woman is thinking? How can she not recognize her own husband simply because he's donned a hat and glasses, colored his face a bit. This is no comic book! This is real life. Could a week have changed him so much? Perhaps we have not imagined things as fully as we should have, or perhaps we simply haven't noticed the depth of the character's change as we've been with him every moment. Whatever the case, she longs for him as she would a stranger she'd met who opened something inside her. Everything about this Dr. Hallen seems so self-assured, she thinks to herself later that morning as she dusts the furniture. Wasn't it something how he offered his hand to her. Like a romantic hero from the movies!

Once safely back inside his new house, Gregory Two barricades himself in the bathroom, takes off his disguise, and scrubs the area we might call his face. He stares into the mirror. *I am married to Mrs. Glob, he says. I have two children and a dog. I garden on Sundays, even though I hate it. I own a house with an acre of land and a beautiful view of oaks and elms in the back. I spend lots of time on my computer looking at nothing then wonder what happened to my day. I take my children to swimming and music. I tuck them in each night and wake them up every morning.* He scrubs again, this time with the hottest water he can stand, then continues this recitation of his habits. *I rise first on weekends and make omelets and pancakes for my family. I clean the toilets each week because no one else will. I look forward to Monday mornings because my cubicle at work is the only place I can hear my own thoughts.* Poor Gregory Two! He tries to remain fixed even as his body cocoons him. It is best we leave him like this for a month or so. The dark and violent churning of the soul is not a pretty sight. Look at him, now, collapsed upon the cold, tile floor. Something a glob would never willingly do. Is that a fetal position he is curled into? It's impossible to tell, but whatever it is, it's unbecoming. Let us go. It's the only decent thing to do, or so we tell ourselves. But you know the truth. You are starting to see through the veneer of our words already. We didn't want it to be this hard, this painful. We'd hoped it would be otherwise.

Early November, and it's getting colder in Ohio. Not a time globs usually enjoy. From November to April, one would usually find Gregory Glob huddled on the couch beneath a pile of electric blankets. But this November Gregory Two sits in the La-Z-Boy that has become his favorite chair and plays Dylan's *The Times They Are A Changin'* with the dexterity and verve of a much younger man. He even adds a closing riff that would make the bard himself jealous. If we examine our Gregory closely, we distinguish a man quite different from the one we left behind only thirty days before. Note the lightness with which he rises from the chair to get himself more coffee. Pay attention to the flash of the eyes as he sets the coffee down and studies the next song in his new *Mel Bay Anthology of Great Folk Hits*, the luster of his brow, as if each thought tinders a flame within. He no longer needs those electric blankets. Watch him long enough to see what we have described, and you will understand this appears no common man. We regret our decision now to leave him. We were frightened. We admit it. Metamorphosis is a violent thing. Can you blame us for turning away? And yet, what we wouldn't give for a glimmer of that vision now, just enough to light our own path, enough to believe that such change is possible. Only yesterday we told our piano teacher we needed to quit. We said money was a problem, but we knew the real reason. It was so difficult to make the lessons, to step outside of our routine. Worse still was practicing. Adults shouldn't be made to face failure on a daily basis.

After deciding on the next song he'll learn in the Dylan canon with the self-assurance of a veteran making out the encore list for his reunion tour, our dear Gregory once again sips his coffee and recalls the past few visits to his neighbor, Mrs. Glob. Yes, a month can be an eternity when a body, even a glob body, undergoes such a sudden and all encompassing transformation. Gregory Two has completely forgotten his old life. His dear Jane has been reduced in his mind to the neighbor, Mrs. Glob. To say "reduced" may be too strong a term as he finds he enjoys his neighbor's company very much. Far more than he ever enjoyed the company of his wife. In fact, their talks over coffee each Thursday morning have extended into lunch. She makes him laugh. Something he's not sure he's ever really been good at before. She says he makes her laugh, too. And he knows it's true because he feels the warmth of her smile as they sit in front of the bay window in the kitchen, each sipping their coffee, occasionally allowing one hand to graze that of the other as they reach for their cups. He can't remember how it all began. He vaguely recalls that first awkward meeting when he broke the vase, then not much after. Only that he'd made some pretense to see her the following week. The next meeting didn't go much better. He'd stood on the doorstep, silence shifting awkwardly between them until he made an excuse once again to leave. It was then she confessed that she'd been having trouble sleeping, that her ears would ring at night keeping her up. He told her he'd be happy to examine her if she invited him in for coffee. The rest, as they say, is history. He never did find any evidence that would support the ringing in her ears, and she didn't complain of it again.

Through the living room window, he sees her husband leaving for work and knows it is time for his weekly meeting with Mrs. Glob. To be on the safe side, he checks the street for roving police cars. He'd only eaten one other realtor who'd checked on the property two weeks before, but with three realtors disappearing in a little over a month the police had become suspicious. At first they'd set up a surveillance, which was easy enough for a glob to avoid, but now things seemed to have calmed down. He'd seen no sign of the cops in a few days. And there'd been no more realtors. He had a feeling they'd already written the house off as a loss and were staying away.

He dons his glasses and hat and walks to his neighbor's house two doors down, whistling to himself all the while. She gestures him in and pours him a cup of coffee, as is her habit. They make small talk, chatting about her children, how the oldest, Elizabeth, or Liza as she calls her, is starting to separate, to assert her own identity. How sad she is that her daughter doesn't seem to need her as much. The younger, Henry, seems to be growing depressed, retreating further and further into his imagination. She doesn't understand this and finds when she tries to talk with her husband about it, he dismisses her. She rarely mentions her husband in their Thursday morning conversations, and so when she does, she looks down at her coffee and takes a slow sip, perhaps wishing she'd not brought him up.

"I understand," Gregory Two says. He takes her hand in his. She looks to him like a startled bird, but she does not pull her hand away. "Your husband is a lucky man," he says. "He doesn't realize how lucky."

"You must have many female admirers, doctor," she replies. "You're handsome. Intelligent." His strawberry Jell-O skin blushes pale.

"Call me, Tom," he says, as he leans in closer. "And you're the only patient I care to see."

He kisses her. Wouldn't it be wonderful if he kissed her eyes? We've always wanted to kiss someone on the eyes. It is not all about leaving. Some of us understand this. Yes, to leave our wives, our jobs, our families. That takes courage. But there are those of us who argue it takes more courage to stay. To stay and kiss your wife on the eyes. Poppycock! we want to tell them. It takes nothing to stay. And we are right. They know it, and we know it. But what goes unspoken, what we fear to mention even to each other is the kind of courage it takes to stay and change our habits. To stay and risk everything.

Yes, he kisses her eyes. We've decided. He moves to her mouth, but instead of kissing her lips, he whispers to her: *O, this is the animal that never was.* Rilke! There is nothing more romantic than that! This is much better than we could have imagined. It's such a treat when scenes take on a life of their own! He embraces her, and they kiss again. He whispers another line between her lips. *It had not been. But for them it appeared in all its purity.* She gives him a puzzled look, as if reconsidering whether to have an affair with this strange man. But he pulls her to him so tightly she couldn't get away even if she'd wanted. Yes! Yes! Take her the way she yearns to be taken! Take her on the kitchen table. On the floor. Hold her close against you. Kiss her passionately, Gregory Two! Kiss her lips, her neck, her shoulders! If only we could do that, we wouldn't be here now, writing this. Learn from our mistakes, dear Gregory!

"You excite me, Tom," she whispers back. Her eyes wide. "You make me so happy."

Even our highly trained imaginations have difficulty describing the physical gymnastics of the next scene, what with a glob and a human fused together the way they were, rolling over the furniture, falling off the kitchen table, smashing against the refrigerator. Under the best of conditions, picturing the sex lives of others is never advisable, and when it involves two different species, it's really best to leave it alone completely. It's for very good reason even the greatest writers avoid sex scenes. What we can say is that it was a passion of which neither of them had ever dreamed. They opened to each other. Exposed their fears, their most vulnerable selves. Even now we feel as if we're almost there with them. As if their love carved out a space for us. It's intoxicating... to be loved in that way. We'll never forget it. It doesn't even matter if actual intercourse took place. That's merely physical. And this was so much more. What is important is that for an hour or so their bodies seemed to be one. In several instances, it appeared as if Gregory Two, or should we now say Tom, attempted to pull back and finish the poem he'd begun. But he'd scarcely get a word out before she'd pull him to her once again. At last, when the two of them lie side by side, sweating and sprawled upon the oak kitchen floor, he finishes the poem. *It drew near to a virgin, white, gleaming—and was, inside the mirror and in her.*

"Yes, Tom," she says, as they fall asleep in each other's arms, dreaming of the shape of that thing they created between them. And then he lays his hand on her chest.

We recognize, dear reader, that at this point you

are probably quite skeptical. When did Tom, we mean Gregory Two, ever show an inkling toward poetry? Just because he takes up folk music doesn't mean this petty bourgeois man starts spouting Rilke! You are right to be skeptical. Of course, this characteristic says more about us than about him. We hope by now you are starting to understand. We fear to do so many things. To act is so much more difficult than to write. And so we hope you forgive us these small intrusions, these moments when our own desires bleed into the actions of our characters. We never know what scenes our mind will pull up like a catfish from the deepest regions of our psyche. The last words of that poem and then the way he touched her, as if he really knew her. We haven't cried like that while writing in as long as we can remember. It's unprofessional, we know. We wish we could say it won't happen again. But we don't care. Gregory Two is a courageous man. He is choosing to live a life of passion, and we worship him.

The second such encounter occurred the following day and went very much like the first. He holds her after, raining kisses on her, feeling like a god. He tries to remember the last time he's felt this way but can recall nothing. In fact, he realizes with not a little trepidation, his memories begin with the moment he sat in the La-Z-Boy in the open house he took over on 116 Joy Lane. Surely, he must have known others, must have had many previous relationships. He searches his memory even as she lies snoring next to him on the living room floor, her head resting against her son's Lego castle. An image flashes through his mind of a woman he might have known, one he'd cared for, he thinks. The image is too vague to be called a memory. But in it he thinks he sees

29

two young children running toward a mound pulsating on the ground, some sort of gelatinous mass. They never arrive. Who are they? he asks. And who do they run to? He tries to focus in on the figures, but the more intensely he thinks about it, the fuzzier it all gets. As quickly as it comes, the image is gone, and he's left shaking on the living room floor. He curls next to Jane. "Run away with me," he whispers in her ear. Our hearts nearly stop at the beauty of these words.

She wakes and turns to him, her wide eyes inches from his face. "I can't change my life like that," she whispers.

If we could slap her we would. But of course, we have so little control over the unfolding situation. It's really quite painful to be able to do nothing but watch as a character ruins her life. All because of a lack of vision of what is possible! Only a little while before she stood on tiptoe, stretching out to him, yearning to follow him anywhere, and now he offers her the chance at a life of passion!

"Why not?" he pulls her to him, feeling desire once again course through his ovoid bulk. But this time she moves away.

"Look around," she says as she stands. "I've made a life here." She grabs framed photos one after another off the mantle. "Do you see my kids?"

Don't do it Gregory Two! Not even Odysseus had to face such temptations! We have no wax with which to seal your eyes.

"Yes," he replies, though he remains prostrate on the floor. She kneels beside him, shoves picture after picture in his face.

"Here's one of the day we moved to Ohio."

"Everyone looks so happy."

"Yes," she replies. "The kids ran screaming with joy from the car when they saw our new yard." She shoves another picture in his face.

"Who is that?" he asks.

"It's my husband.

"Oh."

"What? You didn't expect him to look like that?"

"I don't know what I expected."

"You should know what the man looks like whose wife you're sleeping with."

Gregory Two takes the picture. "He looks like a nice enough guy. A bit doughy about the middle."

"He's a good glob," she replies. "He doesn't deserve this." She pauses, her eyes gazing somewhere beyond him. "What are we going to do?"

The sound of a car pulling into the driveway answers her question. Mrs. Glob runs to the window. "My God, it's him. My husband!"

Gregory Two stands but drops the picture. It bounces on the Berber carpet, breaking the frame. He tries to kick it under the sofa but can't, not having any feet. He pounces on it and dissolves it instead, then heads for the kitchen, hoping to make it out the back door.

"There's no time!" Mrs. Glob shouts as the key clicks in the lock. "Quick! In the pantry!"

Gregory Two oozes under the closed pantry door just as the front door opens and Gregory One steps inside. "Honey, I've got some news," he says as he pours himself a coffee and sits at the kitchen table.

Mrs. Glob tries to pour her own cup but pours so

much that when she adds milk it spills over the counter. "You seem so excited," she attempts to say calmly. "What's going on?"

"I quit my job today," he says.

We did not foresee this. Not at all. There have been so many surprises during the writing of this story, we are starting to doubt our own ability to imagine this through to the end. Still, we press on. It's all we can do.

Mrs. Glob reaches for a towel to clean the mess but stops. "You're scaring me, dear." She sits at the table. "What are you saying?"

"I quit," he replies. "From this day forward I'm a new man."

The words hit Gregory Two like a fire extinguisher (the CO2 kind), and he recoils to the back pantry like he did the night he tried to eat those people trapped in the storage cellar of the diner all those years ago. Now he is the one trapped, and he doesn't like it one bit. He doesn't dare open the door for fear the hinges might squeak. So he sits in the darkness surrounded by several boxes of cereal—he can smell the Honey Nut Cheerios (his favorite), can see the faint outline of cans of cream of mushroom soup (Who eats that?), can feel the large bag of basmati rice pushing against his back (Why would someone buy so much rice?). The entire panorama of food plays on his senses until he's no longer sure where he is. In fact, as he sits in the darkness, he almost feels as if it's his voice talking to Jane out in the kitchen. If he concentrates hard enough, he can almost guess the husband's words before he utters them. It's eerie, in fact, how similar those words seem to something he might say himself.

"I've been unsatisfied," he says. "I didn't realize how much until today."

"What do you mean?" Mrs. Glob asks. Gregory Two can imagine her hand shaking as she smoothes out her skirt, the very skirt he'd removed a mere hour before. "Unsatisfied with what?"

"With everything."

"Does that include our marriage?"

"We can be better, Jane," he says.

A fire burns in Gregory Two's nose and mouth. Are there jalapeños hanging above him? Did they brush against his face? No, it's cayenne pepper. That has to be what's dusting the floor. The pantry is a mess. He had no idea Jane was such a poor housekeeper.

"I don't know if I want us to be better," Jane replies. "I liked things just the way they were."

How can she say this when not half an hour before she was making love to the man she thinks is her neighbor? Can she be so out of touch with her own feelings? Of course, we know the answer to this as soon as we ask it. We wouldn't be writing this now if we were in touch with our own feelings. We wouldn't be doing most of the things that fill our days: sleeping, surfing the Internet, watching sports, movies, reality TV, entertaining ourselves into a stupor. We should be more careful of the questions we ask.

"The past few weeks I've felt a sea change coming," he goes on as if he hasn't heard. "It's been building up. I thought at first I might lose my mind. I thought I might split down the middle. I didn't know what it was until today."

"I don't like this talk," Jane says. Gregory Two

imagines her trying to stand, to walk away. He sees the husband grab her by the hand, pull her to him as he stands. He feels certain they are kissing passionately at this very moment. The thought drives him wild. He shifts about the pantry, stirring up the cayenne pepper or whatever it is until he's choking on it. He can barely breathe. The pepper works its way into his nose now, and he fights back a sneeze.

"We're going to live differently," the husband continues.

Oh sure! Gregory Two thinks. This guy waltzes in here, kisses the woman I've fallen in love with, and starts spewing out vague statements like "live differently!" That's just... Ah! Ah! Ah.......chooooo!"

"What was that?" the husband asks. Gregory Two swells like a puffer fish. He's ready for a fight, either that or it's the jalapeños.

"I love your voice," Jane says. "There is something different about it."

"I'm still here, Jane. But I'm not the man I was."

"Yes, I can see it's you," Jane replies. "But it's not. The way you hold yourself is different."

"Kiss me," he says. "Kiss me again and again."

Gregory Two swells so much he knocks over the cans of cream of mushroom. He is sure he'll be discovered and waits at the ready. But nothing happens. After several minutes of silence, he dares to ooze a bit under the door and take a peek. They are gone.

"Yes! Yes! Yes!" Jane's screams of pleasure sound from upstairs. Each scream coldly familiar. He sees the bedroom in his mind's eye. He can imagine exactly how the husband pins her against the wall, kissing the back of her neck. How he moves against her even as he stares at the picture of the two of them on the bedside table: in the photo, Jane gazes into her husband's eyes as if he is her entire world, and he smiles back at her as if she, too, is the only place he wants to be. Gregory Two sees how in their passion they knock over the pile of books on the bedside table, books the husband has meant to read but never found the time for: Tolstoy and Chekhov, and Flaubert. It's only when he imagines the blank journal lying in the closed bedside table drawer that he shakes so violently he nearly splits a second time. And what would we do with yet another Gregory to follow? It would be too much. Thankfully he maintains the presence of mind to get out of the house and roll quickly down the street only to hide once again in the comforting habits of his new life.

Once home, he swats the Mel Bay guitar book from the music stand, then takes the guitar by the neck and raises it above his head. He stands before the fireplace ready to smash it down. Who is this glob who thinks he can change his life so easily without changing the outer trappings of that life? He doesn't understand why he feels so insulted by this, but he does. It's a slap in the face to anyone who takes change seriously, to anyone who believes it takes work. He raises the guitar higher still, not sure why he needs to smash it down. End it now, he thinks, before you find out the truth. And it's the acknowledgment of this deeper truth, this locked door inside him that remains closed despite the violent changes he's endured that sets him to hyperventilate. He sits back in the La-Z-Boy and cradles the guitar tightly to his chest. I am more, he says to himself. I am more than this. But he still can't breathe, and so he plays a song he knows will soothe him. *Knockin' on Heaven's Door.* A simple song. One he could play in his sleep. The repetitive lyrics and chord patterns calm his nerves until he dozes off for the rest of the afternoon in the chair, the guitar resting on his lap.

He wakes to the sound of an electric edger. Sleepily, he rises and peers out the living room window toward his neighbor's house. Mr. Glob is edging his lawn! It's dusk, and he's edging his lawn! Look how he kneels and sights the line like a golfer before the winning putt. He even goes back over the edge to make sure he's got a clean line. Gregory Two must admit it looks impressive. Better still, perhaps this means his neighbor isn't so serious about changing his life. What's he doing now? Fertilizing! My God! It's not even spring! Who fertilizes in November? Yes! This is a very good sign. Who makes big life changes while caring so desperately for their lawn? This should be good, he thinks, then backs away from the window, grabs his hat and glasses, and opens the front door.

Jane stands beside her husband admiring the lawn. He takes a deep breath, then heads toward them. "Howdy, neighbors!" he says. "Beautiful evening, isn't it?"

Jane steps back, visibly shaken, but recovers. "Dear, this is the new neighbor I've told you about. Dr. Hallen."

"Call me, Tom." Gregory Two extends what appears to be a hand, which is met by Gregory One's own greeting appendage. "A firm handshake, I see," Gregory Two says, not letting go.

"Yours, too," Gregory One replies. "You must work out."

"I write lots of prescriptions. It keeps the hand

muscles strong."

Neither of them lets go. In fact, if either had bones, they'd be bruised or crushed by now. Note, too, how fully Gregory Two has absorbed his new life. He actually believes himself to be a doctor, though he has yet to see a patient. Few traces if any of his old life remain.

Attempting to ease the tension, Jane rests a hand on each of them and invites them for a drink. "It's such a lovely evening," she says. "It's a shame not to enjoy it." Neither moves, so Jane ushers them both to the porch. "You two have a seat," she says, gesturing to the only furniture on the porch: a two-seater swing. She disappears inside, and the two are left staring at the swing, then at each other.

"I see you'd both rather stand than relax," Jane says when she returns. She sets two of the beers on the table next to the swing. "Suit yourselves." She sits and sips her beer.

Gregory One moves to sit beside her just as Two does the same. They bump into each other and pull back. They eye each other a moment, then repeat the process until finally they tumble over each other, squishing into the swing. Jane has to scoot until she is pressed against the side. Although their lower bodies mold to the limited space, their upper bodies ooze out in all directions. It feels to Gregory Two as if he were sitting in those tiny airplane seats, his body spilling over onto the guy in the next seat whose own body isn't exactly staying confined to his seat either.

"Well, this is cozy," Jane says, taking a much bigger swig of beer.

Gregory One, who is sitting to her left, attempts to reach his own beer but can't turn enough in his seat to get his arm around. Jane hands both beers to him, and he cups them in his fists as if they were his last, treasured possession.

"Dear, you're being rude," Jane says, nudging him. "Dr. Hallen looks thirsty."

"Please, call me Tom," Gregory Two says, as he pries the beer from One's fist.

"Warm, just the way I like it," Gregory Two says after taking a long swig.

"We don't believe in refrigeration in this house," Gregory One replies, and for a moment the two smile at each other. They actually converse about the weather, the price of real estate and gas. It's only when Gregory Two asks One what he does for a living that the swing starts to rock a little faster. "I'm in between things right now," One replies. "I'm looking for a change. Examining my options."

"It seems to me you've got your life in order," Two says. "You have a beautiful wife, if you don't mind my saying, two wonderful children, and a lovely house. From the outside, it looks pretty good."

"Yes," One says. "Everything's in order." He kicks off the ground with his feet, making the swing arc back so that they nearly fall out.

"Gregory!" Jane scolds. "We're going to need seatbelts in this thing."

"What about you?" One asks Two. "What do you do with all that spare time? No kids. No wife to tie you down."

"Oh, a little of this. A little of that," Two replies, feeling as if he has the upper hand, if that expression can be used with a glob.

One downs his beer. "You must have something that excites you," he says. "A doctor is a profession like any other. What do you want to do? What calls to you from deep inside?"

"I'm not sure what you mean," Two replies, wanting to see how long he can play this game, to see if he can draw the other out before pouncing on him. "What about you? Surely a glob like you must have passions?"

"Well, that's just it," Gregory One begins. "I've lived my entire life just trying to do what was expected. I never really gave a thought to my own feelings, my own needs. To be honest, I didn't know I could.'

The answer is not what Gregory Two expects. He doesn't want to hear that his neighbor has yearnings and desires, a complicated internal life. He wants him to be a mere creature of habit. No, he does not like this at all. It stirs too many feelings inside. So many, in fact, that he kicks the swing into high gear.

"I'm feeling a bit nauseous," Jane says. "Can we slow down?" The two globs ignore her.

"Having a passion isn't something you simply decide on," Two begins. "It has to rise out of you, naturally." He's stumped him, he thinks. He'll show him for the fool he is, and then Jane will be his for the taking.

"I've never believed that hullabaloo that the artist is someone special," One counters as if Two's barb had barely pricked his skin. "I believe whatever a glob sets his mind to he can achieve."

"How American of you," Two retorts, but One keeps talking over him.

"Change the outer man and you'll change what's inside." One slaps Two on the back. "You don't need to know what your passion is, you simply need to alter the details of your life."

"You make it sound so easy," Two replies. "As if you just decide to open the door and let what's inside come out."

"Yes, that seems to be about it."

"What if you open the door and there's nothing inside?" Two asks, surprising himself and us. He's not sure he likes the sound of what he said, nor is he exactly sure what he meant. He'd only wanted to get at his neighbor, to make him think twice about his foolish attempts at change.

The swing rocks violently as One and Two take turns pushing it to greater and greater heights. Jane holds her empty beer bottle in one hand and grips the metal rail of the swing with the other.

"Of course there's something inside," One replies. "That's my point! We've all got the potential. We just need to set the conditions to let it out."

Two represses the desire to punch his neighbor. That would set him back to the beginning of this game he's now found himself in. He opts instead for a final verbal joust. "You can decorate a closet all you want, but it will still be a closet."

The swing stops dead. Jane nearly falls out. Gregory One stands and steps away. "That's preposterous!" he exclaims. "That's why I'm changing jobs, changing my life, changing the beer I drink for Christ's sake. What kind of beer is this, Jane? It's simply awful."

"It used to be your favorite." She looks hurt.

"Not anymore!" he continues. "From now on, it's only European beers. I don't care whether we can afford it or not. And none of that cheap coffee in the morning, either. I want to grind my own beans. I want a French press."

"I thought your coffee was quite good myself," Two exclaims, risking a quick glance at Jane. Luckily, One is much too involved in his own moment to hear.

"I want to get the *New York Times* instead of the local dribble we read. I want to buy my clothes at the Thrift store. Isn't that where artists buy their clothes? I want a motorcycle. Yes! A black Triumph, or a red Indian. One of those classic bikes that turns heads. Not a Harley. God, no! I don't want to become one of those bearded, fat, tattooed men riding out of their middle-aged crises on an obnoxiously loud bike!"

Gregory Two stands as well. The latent feelings of a lifetime threatening to break out of his feeble head. The miserable nature of his life is nearly revealed to him. He's been there. He knows. He felt it today as he held the guitar aloft ready to smash it. He knows what he saw inside himself in that moment, though he fears to admit it. The possibility that he'd opened the door, and there was nothing. His neighbor will never understand because he can't get past the surface. He wants to shout at One, to tell him he has it all wrong. He can almost taste the words about to tumble out of him. If he could just have a moment more, he could savor the sip of an answer tickling his tongue, but the words turn to bile, and he throws up his beer all over One's shirt.

"Of all the crazy....." One begins, but cannot finish. It's as if the words have turned sour in his mouth as well.

Jane jumps up and runs to the kitchen for towels. By the time she returns, dabbing them over her husband,

Gregory Two is making excuses about the lateness of the hour and the fact that he has work to do early the next morning. He apologizes for his sickness, explaining that he's never been good riding on things in motion: cars, trains, planes, porch swings. Gregory One absently says goodbye, then takes the towels and cleans himself. Two risks a final glance at Jane as he shuffles down the sidewalk, but she seems to be looking at neither her husband nor him. If he had to guess, he would say her gaze was fixed on the space between.

That night as he lies in bed, Gregory Two whispers his love for Jane over and over to himself, swearing that if only he could remove that idiot Gregory from the situation, he could have her once again and be happy. Perhaps they would even marry. He could be the father of those two lovely children. They deserved a good father. A better life than what that man could give them. Poor Gregory! He has no idea he desires the very life he gave up. The madness of it makes our head spin.

The next morning he returns once again to his guitar. This time choosing to work on *Scarborough Fair*, something much more difficult. Maybe I haven't been pushing myself enough, he thinks. Maybe I just need to open up, and let things flow. He gives himself a half hour to work out the opening sequence, then gives up and makes himself a pot of coffee. Why don't I have any patients? he wonders. If I'm a doctor, I should be taking care of people. Perhaps I'm one of those doctors like Chekhov or Somerset Maugham, one of those doctors who sees patients only rarely because he is devoted to his art. He spends the morning instead rummaging through the closets looking for a medical bag or any other evidence

42

of his profession. It is only after lunch that he remembers he wanted to learn *Scarborough Fair*. But when he sits down to play, he is disturbed by the roar of a motorcycle prowling up and down the street in front of his house.

"That bastard!" he says as he moves to the window. "A black Triumph! He doesn't waste any time." He opens the front door. "Nice bike..."

Gregory One stops in front of Two's house. "Not bad, huh?"

"It's the cat's meow," Two says. "You'll be the talk of the town."

"I just want to change things up, you know?" One revs the engine for emphasis.

"Nothing like a Triumph to do that," Two replies. "That should open that door inside you to . . . something."

One shoots Two a look, as if he's not sure he's just been insulted. "I was thinking of heading down to the Thrift store. Care to take a ride?" He revs the engine once again.

"No, thanks," Two replies. "I've got to get back to work." He waves goodbye and turns without waiting for a reaction. He doesn't need to. He hears the mis-shift, then the silence as the motorcycle stalls.

Gregory Two pretends to head back up his driveway until the noise from the motorcycle fades down the street, then he doubles back and heads to his neighbor's house. The moment Jane opens the door, he takes her in his arms and carries her to the upstairs bedroom. "The thought of you with that man is driving me crazy!" he says as he unbuttons her blouse. It is here we must point out he is amazingly dexterous for a glob. Note how he unsnaps her bra in one motion as he kisses her. We've

43

always wanted to be able to do that. Whenever we've tried, we end up pinching the girl's skin.

"That man is my husband," Jane replies through heavy panting. "He should be jealous of you! In fact, I should be feeling guilty right now."

"But you're not, are you?" He kisses her, then pushes her down on the bed.

"No, I'm not!" she says, pulling him on top of her. "It's strange. I felt guilty the other day making love to my husband, as if I were betraying you."

"Good." He kisses her neck, her breasts.

"But he's my husband. We've been married nearly thirteen years."

"Then your love is merely habit," he replies. "Now you've moved on." He kisses his way lower still.

"I don't want to change an old habit for a new one," she says, closing her legs on his face. "I want something real."

"But you have something real," he replies, molding his face back to whatever normal is. "We have something real. Can't you feel it?"

She sits up and pulls the pillow to her knees. She lights a cigarette. "You're different from my husband. But my husband is different from my husband now, too."

"Great! I've become the old habit and your husband the new. Is that right?" He takes a cigarette from her pack and lights it. He knows as a doctor he shouldn't smoke, but the need is overwhelming and somehow feels essential to the moment. What sort of man is Gregory? we wonder, that he can pick up new habits without a thought, even ones that are dangerous to him, ones that seem to go against his character.

"I don't know," she says, walking to the window, keeping her back to him. "I'm confused."

"I'll show you I'm the real thing," Gregory Two says, holding his cigarette the way he remembers Bogart holding it in *To Have and Have Not*. He waits for her to sit on his lap like Bacall. She doesn't.

He whistles. Still nothing. He puts out his cigarette and leaves.

Back home, he takes a red pen and puts a big X through *Scarborough Fair*, then turns to *Girl from the North Country* and works determinedly at it all evening. It's slow going at first, but over time he starts to loosen up. He's able not only to find Dylan's unique cadence, but to make it his own. Something about the sound vibrating through the thick, gelatinous goo of his body transforms it into the quintessential rough and ready folksinger's voice, touched with just the right amount of pain. For the first time in several weeks, he sleeps soundly, at least until the roar of the motorcycle cruising up and down the street wakes him.

He jumps from the chair and runs to the window. His nemesis stands, observing his bike in his driveway, dressed in some sort of smoking jacket, black jeans, and pointy-toed shoes. He wears a large satchel, with papers spilling out. A painter's portfolio? The idiot is going to start painting! Gregory Two heads to his neighbor's, but once outside thinks better of it and decides to sneak along the side of the house until he can reach the azaleas for a better look. My God, he's got a piercing! Right through his eyebrow! Gregory One actually sits back on his motorcycle, pulls out a sketchbook and starts drawing. Gregory Two can't believe his eyes. He tries to

45

move closer, hoping somehow he might be able to see a bit of the sketch, to expose his neighbor for the fraud he is! He risks being discovered as he peeps out from the end of the azaleas. He can make out a tree, a few clouds. His neighbor's sketching the horizon! Oh, what a cliché. It's only when Gregory One puts his feet up on the handlebars as he changes to charcoal, and Gregory Two notes the pointy-toed shoes are actually crocodile skin cowboy boots, that he loses it and jumps from the bushes.

"Who are you now, Buffalo Bill?" Two begins. "Or should I say "Crocodile Bill?"

One swivels around in his seat and plants his feet on the ground. "What do you think of my new duds?"

"Isn't it obvious what I think?" Two replies. "Or do your artistic powers of observation not extend that far?" He moves so close to One they can practically absorb each other's skin.

"What's gotten into you?" One tries to stuff the sketchbook back in his satchel but Two grabs it from his hands. "Hey! That's mine," One shouts.

"I'm the artist around here," Two continues. "Not you!"

One reaches for the sketchbook but Two evades his hand. "Funny, I thought you were a doctor. Or are you simply playing doctor?"

"With your wife!" Two replies, shoving the sketchbook in One's face.

For a moment all is still. The front door opens and Jane steps onto the porch wearing a yellow plaid dress just like the one she wore the night she and Gregory first met, the night he almost ate her so long ago when he'd lost himself on that adolescent rampage. "Boys, what's going on?"

She sees the two globs puffed out like two red balloons, the sketchbook held aloft between them. She notes the fierce outline of her husband's face, a look she has not seen before, a look that if she were honest excites her very much. In fact, she is so intoxicated by that look she doesn't see her husband's raised fist until it's too late. Had she been more present, she might have called out a warning and averted the ensuing disaster. Instead, her husband's fist flies with such force it knocks the sketchbook out of Two's hands, the pages of which scatter in the air. The fist continues directly into Two's eye. Obviously, imagining the location of specific details such as an eye (or even the above eyebrow piercing) are difficult, but we do our best. Still, to avoid argument, let's just say the punch landed somewhere around Two's ocular region. In fact, One's fist continued right through Two's ocular region and embedded itself in Two's head. There is always this danger in any glob physical activity, whether it be violence or sexually related. Normally, both globs involved are aware enough to be sure body parts don't become so embedded that they fuse. Unfortunately, that's exactly what happened here.

"Hey!" One shouts. "Give me back my fist!" He makes the natural assumption that Two is consciously choosing to keep the fist sucked inside the gelatinous mass that seems to be his head. If only it were that simple.

"I'm nearly blind, you moron!" Two shouts back. "I've got your fist embedded in my right eye! Take it out, or I'll do the same to you!" He raises his own fist and is about to strike, which would have been a real mess, when Jane runs to the driveway and grabs his arm.

"Boys, please!" she cries. "Calm down!"

"We are calm!" they both shout.

"We've got to think about this," Jane says. "Gregory, why don't you try twisting your hand. You know, the same way you pull a tick out."

Gregory twists and turns but to no avail.

"This is just great!" One exclaims. "How can I paint when this asshole has my hand in his eye!"

"You'll never be an artist now, you son-of-a-bitch!" Two replies. "Just remember that!"

"Be quiet!" Jane shouts. "The both of you are acting like little globkins. Now, here's another idea. Tom, why don't you...."

"Oh, so now you and the doctor are on a first name basis," One says.

"This is not the time, Gregory," Jane puts a hand to his mouth. "Listen, we could try an ice pack. Cold might force each of you to retract enough to free the hand."

"No!" both globs shout. "Let's not get drastic!"

"Then, I suppose you're stuck like this, at least for the time being," Jane replies. She seems almost pleased by the matter.

"Wait just a minute," Two begins. "Where will I live? How will I play my music?"

"Yes, and how can I ride my motorcycle with this chump running along side?" One pipes in.

Jane takes them both by the hand. "We're going to live together in this house, at least until we can sort this out."

It is here we must applaud Jane's ability to adapt to

the given situation. She seems so calm, almost grateful, at such a tense moment. Quite frankly, imagining the scene scared us half to death. All that effort to separate, to start a new life, and for what? It's as if Jane understands something that we don't, as if she knows that things will work out exactly as they're supposed to. Maybe that's what it means to live in the present. People are always telling us: "Live in the present!" But those words seem so empty to a writer. Where is the conflict? The desire? You need the future for that, and a bit of the past, too, just to get a healthy dose of guilt and regret. But it's as if Jane is saying, "Have faith and all will be well!" Where would that leave us? Better to return to what is comfortable. That's all this is. This writing. This working through our own fears and desires. Well, admittedly, it's gone beyond that now. Quite honestly, we're not sure what this is anymore.

The two globs don't speak to each other the rest of the afternoon. Dinner isn't much better. Jane makes each their favorite dish, but macaroni and cheese doesn't mix well with tuna casserole, and all have indigestion after. Then comes the difficulty of sleeping arrangements. At first, One refuses to allow Two anywhere near the bed. Of course, that means he can't be anywhere near the bed either. So, they compromise and push the two twin beds together that they normally reserve for guests. Jane even brings the stack of books from their master bedroom to make it feel more like their normal routine. Then she excuses herself to do her ablutions in the bathroom while Gregory One and Two sit on the edge of the bed staring at each other.

"I always wanted to read Chekhov," Two says. "Just

never had the time."

"Me, too," One replies, picking up the collected stories. He starts thumbing through it.

"I can't see very well," Two says. "Can you read me a few lines?"

One rolls his eyes but opens the book anyway. He reads the first page then starts to fall asleep. The book tips onto One's chest. Two grabs the book and tries to read it but quickly becomes dizzy because his depth perception is off. He sets the book down and looks at One. A vision of himself passes before his eye. He is lying on the bed just as his neighbor is now, an unread book lying beside him. He has tried to read that book before. He looks about the room. It all appears strangely familiar. He knows that dresser, he's almost sure of it. He bought the lamp sitting atop it at a garage sale. He'd been so happy because he nickeled the woman on the price. He lies down, spreads his arms out on the bed to hold himself steady and doesn't dare look about him, his poor brain hopelessly puzzled.

By the time Jane enters, both are asleep. She curls up between them, using her husband's arm as a pillow, thinking life is not so bad. She has her lover and her husband together with her in the same bed. How many girls can say that? She knows it can't last, that the routines of ordinary life must take over eventually no matter how strange the circumstances seem now, and so decides to take full advantage of this new situation.

She pulls Two's arm around her and brings his hand to her mouth. He has no fingers, per se, so she stretches out some digits as one would stretch silly putty, then takes one of the fingers in her mouth. Two's eyes open immediately. "What are you doing, Jane?" he whispers. In answer, she licks his finger up and down. Two groans, then thinks better of it. "We must be careful or we'll wake him," he says.

"I want him awake," Jane replies, moving her foot against One's lower region, carving out a small groove between his legs and nesting her foot there. She moves her foot in and out. One opens his eyes wide. "What are you doing, Jane?" he says.

"I just said that," Two says, pulling his finger from Jane's mouth.

"Boys," Jane replies, grabbing the area where his finger should be and molding it to form a finger once again, then slipping it between her legs. "Tonight marks the start of my new life."

"But, Jane, this is. . . awkward," One protests. "I don't know if I can do it with him here."

"Me, too," Two chimes in. "I mean if it was two women that would be one thing, but two globs?"

Jane bites Two's finger.

"Ouch!"

"It's time for me to take care of myself," Jane says. "I'm doing things differently from now on."

Jane pushes her backside against Two even as she pulls One closer to her. The two globs are hesitant at first. They paw her awkwardly. And heaven forbid if they graze against each other.

"Don't touch me!"

"I didn't touch you. You touched me!"

"I most certainly did NOT!"

But Jane proves to be quite adept at bringing the three together. She stops their fights immediately by

51

making them tend to her. Ever so slowly, she inches them forward, skillfully manipulating each glob so that he can't help but touch the other as he gives her pleasure. Expertly, she wiggles and works her way between them, so that soon each is so lost in his own pleasure that he forgets there even is an other.

Isn't it beautiful? It's moments like this that make our life seem bearable. We wish we could imagine every sordid act for you, but it's better for all if we don't go into the details of what they did that night. Trust us. As pleasant as it seems now, those details will play in your mind. The fact that such connection is possible! It eats away at you in the end. Reminds you of your own loneliness, your own inability to break the patterns that lock you down. Suffice it to say, it proved to be an adventure they would not soon forget, or at least one Jane wouldn't forget, as the moment their lovemaking was over, the two globs began succumbing to their own particular system, to be molded by their own miserable routines.

Lucky for Jane, she left the house early that morning for a pedicure followed by shopping. After arguing about breakfast—Gregory One thought they should ride his motorcycle down to the café in town and do some drawing while Two wanted to grab his guitar and play in the park—they decided on a compromise. They would eat cereal, then pick up Two's guitar before going to the café. This time, as One pours milk on his Wheaties, he's the one who suddenly feels as if he were walking into someone else's dream. The way the milk bounces off the flakes and spatters. There's something familiar in the pattern of the spots of milk on the green tablecloth, something that calls to him from a half-remembered life.

The experience is only exacerbated when little Henry and Elizabeth enter the kitchen, Henry's hair sticking up from his head, as he sleepily pours his own cereal.

The children eat quietly, reading the cereal boxes in front of them. Once finished, they take their bowls to the sink and return to the kitchen table, asking for lunch money, which both One and Two eagerly provide.

"Bye, Dad," they say, giving them each a quick but loving hug. They leave without looking back.

"What do you make of that?" Two asks after the door slams shut.

"I have no idea."

"Well, shall we pick up my guitar?"

"You're going to love the café," One replies, rising to rinse his bowl. "Nothing like a change in routine to get the creative juices flowing."

"I'm worried about the cigarette smoke," Two says, following closely. "What will it do to my voice?"

"It will make it gritty, real!" One replies. "The smell of java. People chatting. Life happening all around you. That's what it's all about." He drags Two down the hallway and opens the closet door.

"No! Not a tweed jacket," Two says. "The clothes don't make the artist and neither does the atmosphere!"

"It may not," One replies. "But anything helps." He dons the jacket, then pulls out a beret.

"Oh my God!" Two shouts. "You're not going to wear that thing, are you?"

"And what's wrong with my hat?"

"You look like an idiot, that's what's wrong!"

"Why do you care what I look like?"

"Because your fist is in my eye! We'll be seen

together!" Two sends out a tendril and anchors it around the kitchen table.

One stretches toward the front door but can't quite reach the knob. "Fine!" he shouts. "Have it your way! We won't go out!" Utilizing the tension from their stretching in opposite directions, One rubber bands back to the kitchen table and morphs himself around the chair so that there is no hope of prying him loose. Two can only stand next to him and watch as One pulls out his sketchbook and begins working.

"Switching to charcoal I see," Two says, attempting to make the best of a difficult situation.

"Yes."

"I like the way you use the eraser to create texture. That's a nice effect."

"Thank you."

"Who are you drawing?" Two goes on. "That's an interesting shape for a figure."

One doesn't answer but instead works even more furiously than before, only stopping occasionally to adjust his beret. Two continues watching, unsure what to do. The more One works, the more Two can't think. He paces and nearly pulls One from his chair.

"Can't you see I'm working here," One says.

"I can barely see at all! That's the point!" Two replies. "It would be nice if I could work, too. Perhaps you would consider going with me to get my guitar." But One is lost in his work and appears to hear nothing.

Two begins pacing again, the arc of his pacing circumscribed by exactly how far he can stretch One without losing his own balance. He paces to the right until he forces One to lean so far over the table that he can no longer see what he's doing. Same to the left. To One's credit, he keeps working. As Two paces, he thinks about the ways in which he'd like to murder One. He sees a ceramic bull atop a knickknack shelf and imagines slamming it down on One's head. Then there's the statue of Don Quixote, complete with sword. Why hadn't he noticed these things before? Where did they come from? He remembers a trip to Spain with Jane and the kids. How is this possible? He sees the children so vividly as they play at the edge of the surf, wanting him to join them in the water. He sees how he sits in the shade to read. He doesn't even like the book he's reading. He tries to read the name of the book, to make out a few of the lines, as if discerning those words might tell him why he is in such a scene. Gregory One yanks him back to the table, and the vision is gone. He is a doctor with dreams of becoming a folksinger. A doctor who is having an affair with his neighbor's wife. A doctor who is inexplicably joined to this imbecile!

Two sits and watches One work. Though One appears to be sketching feverishly, he has actually been shading the same spot over and over so that a dark circle now blots out the figure he'd begun. As the seconds tick by, One slows his pace until he's no longer drawing at all. The two globs stare at the page on the kitchen table until the clock strikes the noon hour. Then, for no apparent reason, Gregory One and Two stand simultaneously, make a sack lunch consisting of a ham sandwich, an apple, and two Oreo cookies, and walk out the door. Only after they've parked the car and walked into the sterile, gray building do they stop and read the sign on the door: "Gregory Glob Insurance." They stand staring at that sign, reading it over and over, as if they can't comprehend its simple message. The human soul truly is a far country, and the soul of a glob is, perhaps, even farther. We've been doing our best to imagine them since we started this story, and still we understand so little of their behavior. Barely a fraction. In short, the events of the last month have confused us utterly. Why, it's as if neither Gregory One nor Two understands what he does, as if neither is much different from the amoeba from which he supposedly evolved. Where is the awareness of self we thought was fundamental to all higher beings? We've devoted our days and nights to imagining these events, and yet we have so little to show for it. All we can do is follow Gregory One and Two as they slump home, hating their puny lives and their own inability to rise beyond them.

Davey greets them, tail wagging, when they pull into the driveway. We've said little about the dog, as there is little to say. He is a black lab, typical in all respects, and he is starting to gray around the collar, though to look at him now he appears like a puppy, his whole body wagging as he carries his squeaky, stuffed squirrel in his mouth. He wants to play. He greets Gregory this way each day when he returns from work, just as he greets the kids when they come home from school, or Jane when she returns from her errands. No matter who it is, he runs to them, with his toy in his mouth. Look at him now as he drops the toy in front of Gregory One and Two, waiting for them to play with him. They shuffle on past, and Davey picks up his toy and follows, still hopeful. He'll do the same with the kids in an hour and repeat it again tomorrow and the next day, even though the last time someone took the stuffed squirrel and threw it for him was two years before.

Gregory One and Two pick up the paper from the porch, go inside and sit on the living room couch to read. They fight over the sports section, finally agreeing to alternate between the sports and the comics. Jane is upstairs dressing in her sexiest negligee, hoping for a repeat of the night before. She walks slowly down the staircase, her hand gliding along the banister. She stops midflight, waiting for them to notice her. But neither looks in her direction. She clears her throat, then proceeds to walk her sexiest walk down the remainder of the stairs. Neither raises his head.

"Excuse me," she says. "Boys." Still nothing.

She enters the living room, "I'm so cold in this little old nightgown," she says. "I was wondering if one of you boys could start a fire. Gregory One and Two each reluctantly sets down his section of the paper, then One takes the real estate section and crumples it up for kindling while Two prepares the logs. The fire roars to flame almost immediately. In the warm glow, they see the grotesque shadow of dear Jane bending down beside them, trying to give them the best view of her cleavage. It is as if the whole of their lives unfolds in that shadow, the entire monotonous routine playing out before them: returning home from work, briefcase in hand, to a peck on the cheek from Jane; sitting on the living room sofa with the evening paper while Jane fetches the slippers; attempting to have a conversation about their day as the kids finish their homework at the kitchen table; tucking the kids into bed, then reaching for a glass of whiskey instead of for Jane; sitting once again at the living room sofa, staring into the fire until it's time for bed.

Jane approaches, wraps them in her arms, puckers her lips for a kiss, but both Gregory One and Two push her away.

"What's the matter, baby?" she says, teasing the negligee down over her breast with her finger.

The flames flicker in the fireplace, coloring Gregory One and Two blood red. *Run!* we want to shout. *Get out while you can!* But of course we don't. All we can do is let events unfold as imagination requires. We sit powerless as Jane foolishly tries once again to bring the globs together, not understanding the self-loathing worming inside of each at that very moment. She reaches for One's hand, takes it to her breast, trying to make things right. The globs pulse dangerously. "Isn't it about time you boys accepted one another?" she asks, slipping between them.

We want to say we never expected this. That we hoped for something better. But that wouldn't be completely true. The memory of the night they shared together still plays in our minds, reminding us of the beauty they almost had, the beauty we don't dare even to imagine. Yes, if we are completely honest, we must say deep down inside part of us wanted this to happen. So, when we say that we can't bear to continue, that we only keep writing because we must, because it's our job, you must take it with a heavy dose of salt. Remember, we who imagine for a living are human, too.

The two globs lunge upon her, enveloping Jane in one swift motion, pulsating over her as they work to dissolve her skin, to absorb her blood and bones into their own body. By the time they are done, Gregory One and Two have fused completely together. We try to look for telltale signs of where one of them ends and the other begins, but it is simply impossible. Not a line or seam remains to mark their former selves. In fact, if anything, we'd say that this new, united glob is even more globlike than before. Perhaps it is because he's so recently gorged himself, but his pallor is redder of hue, his texture a more robust gelatin.

The next morning, the children make it off to school without a hitch. Thank goodness! At least they're okay. We must say, we had our worries, but they are self-sufficient little tykes. They pass through the hallway, lunchboxes in hand, not even stopping to notice their father, pulsating in the living room, slightly larger than they'd remembered him. Had the dog been barking, they surely would have stopped to see what was the matter, or at the very least to give their father a hug goodbye. But strangely, Davey is nowhere to be found. We refuse to imagine what may have happened to that poor dog.

Gregory seems confused as he shambles about the living room, oozing over the sofa, then glomming onto the window, then trying to squeeze through the vent, and finally returning to his original spot where he pulsates in the middle of the carpet. At last, he grabs his briefcase and hat from the entryway and opens the door as if on his way to work, as he'd done every morning until that fateful day several weeks ago now.

Here is where we must leave him, as he stands hesitant in the open doorway, half of him remaining in the shade of the house, the other half under the early morning sunlight. Leave him in the way we are so afraid to leave anything else in our lives. Why is it we can take action here inside the story and not where it really counts? We ask this question even as we know the answer. It is so easy to hide in the recesses of the imagination, to shape the story the way we want it to be, to let others make the difficult decisions while we linger on, working through the daily routine of our humdrum lives. We who refuse to leave the warm embrace of habit. We who cannot face the horror of a broken routine. We who shackle ourselves to others so that they may never feel the possibility our poor Jane and Gregory felt that one sumptuous night.

No! We simply can't bear to go on. Imagination no longer provides the sanctuary we seek. It no longer provides respite from the violent contortions of the soul we sought so desperately to avoid. So, we leave you with the final report from the Granville Gazette about Gregory's last rampage through the neighborhood, how after eating everything in sight, he grew so large he girdled the entire town of Granville. This time, they left him in the arctic without chance of parole. The judge even attached a provision that denied Gregory time off for possible, future good behavior. Some offenses are unpardonable, the judge was quoted as saying, and Gregory's crime, a crime against the self, was the most heinous of all! It's really quite sad. You can understand why we couldn't continue. Poor, dear Gregory! He worked so hard at change. But in the end he simply traded out the trappings of one life for another, never really looking at the glob within, not quite strong enough to see how malleable that glob is, how it's always shifting and changing, always on the verge of becoming.

THE SECRET LIVES OF ACTORS

Each night when he returns home from rehearsal, he cuts off a finger. He takes the scissors from the medicine cabinet in the bathroom, sits on the stool, leans over the tub, and *clip, clip!* There's no blood because he has none. But he leans over the tub anyway to catch the few drops of juice that trickle out. Cupping the finger in his palms, he carries it out the back door, walks slowly down the porch steps, then kneels in the center of his garden, digs a small hole, lays the finger inside and covers it with a mix of dirt and fertilizer, patting it down gently. He hates working with a new moon. All that fumbling around, trying to find the spade in the dark. He stepped on the hoe last time, and it flipped up and whacked him in the face. Since then, he's been careful to hang all the tools in the shed and keep a flashlight on the porch. Once he has it buried, he returns to his kitchen and pulls a small Tupperware container of blood from the fridge. He won't need all of it. But better to be safe than sorry. He drips a few drops onto the newly planted finger and waits, barely breathing, watching the blood soak into the dirt. It's the same each night, except for the fact that he alternates fingers. Monday it's the thumb; Tuesday, the index finger; Wednesday, the middle finger; Thursday, the ring; Friday, it's the pinkie, which rarely works out well. Then he has to suffer through Saturday and Sunday not because he couldn't start back in again on his thumb, which grows back rather quickly, but because the process

63

simply gets to be too much. It really is exhausting, and he's learned if he's to have any hope at all, he needs a couple days rest.

He stands on the porch now and shines the light over the garden. Last night's finger has nearly grown. It was the index wasn't it? If he wasn't so tired of it all, he would say it's beautiful. Seven-feet tall. Topped with red hair. A slight orange tint to the skin, but nothing too unnatural. Dare he say it, a handsome face. A Clark Gable face. Fully articulated arms and legs. Like looking in a mirror. The spitting image of dear old dad. The figure opens its mouth, stretching, as if it might say something. *This time I will not disappoint you. This time you'll know what it's like to love. This time she will know who you are.* Or, maybe it would simply remind him of the time. Nearly midnight. He better hurry. He returns to his house and cleans out last night's ashes from his rather large fireplace. When he's swept every corner clean, he piles on the logs and lights a new fire, then strips off his clothes. Before he climbs inside, he lifts a picture from the mantle that has been laid face down. He gazes into the dark eyes and whispers her name before placing the picture back on the mantle the same way he found it. *Nikki.* He crawls into the fireplace. Just in time! he thinks as the flames engulf him.

By dawn, when the fire is reduced to burning coals and the old Thing to cinders and ash, the new Thing reaches down and tears the tendril of root from its ankle, then steps free of the garden. To all intents and purposes it looks and acts exactly like the old Thing, whose name was Jim. Therein lies the problem. The new Thing--whose name is also Jim—enters the living room and dresses in the same blue jeans and button up flannel left by his predecessor. He then stands before the mirror in the entry and thinks the saddest thoughts he can summon. He imagines the little girl he never had, how she'll die of Leukemia at age six, how he'll kneel by her bedside, holding her hand as she whispers "I love you, Daddy," with her last breath. He checks the mirror for any sign of watery eyes, a quivering lip, even tense lines about the mouth. Nothing. He imagines the mother of the same girl having an affair. He pictures himself walking in on her as she sits naked on top of another man in his own bed, even while their own daughter lies dying of cancer in the hospital. He watches his wife riding up and down on this man. He waits for the anger to rise within. Perhaps if he were to get his body into it, he might feel something. He takes an umbrella from the shelf in the entry closet and holds it as if it were a club. He then grabs a pillow from the living room couch and sets it atop the decorative console beneath the entry mirror. He raises the umbrella above his head and slams it down over and over on the pillow. It makes an impressive *thwack,* as he imagines bludgeoning the man in the head as the man makes love to his wife. He stops, looks in the mirror for the slightest trembling of his brow, for any sign of a scowl upon his lips. Still Nothing. He closes one eye and raises the eyebrow of the other, giving himself the angriest look he can muster. It looks menacing enough. Downright scary, he thinks. But in his body, he feels nothing. What about happy? It's far easier to smile than to frown, right? He imagines now the same six year old girl free of cancer, jumping up from her bed and hugging him, squeezing him for all he's worth, telling him over and over how much she loves him, how happy she is to be alive. He looks in the mirror. He may as well be dead! Maybe it's the fact that he's summoning false memories. What about a real one? Yes! What should be the happiest memory of his life? The one memory that would clearly show he can feel. The first time he talked to Nikki.

They were at a party celebrating the opening of the new theatre season. He'd had to force himself to talk with her. She held the room, surrounded by men. How would he ever have a chance? Yes, he remembers now. He waited until midnight, hoping the room would clear, but the men never left her orbit. It was now or never, so he walked right up to her and asked her a question: "What do you think is the secret of acting?" Curiosity, she'd said, and that answer had surprised him. Curiosity and obsession. You have to want more than anything to understand what makes other people tick. You have to have a deep desire to get inside others. The rest of the party ceased to exist. He and Nikki stepped to a corner and talked together until the host kicked them out. Then they simply walked about the city talking through the night. He remembers her face tilted toward him, how it seemed as if he was her entire world. She paid no attention to where she was walking. He had to pull her from the street several times as an oncoming car was about to hit her.

When morning came, they continued their talk at a café while the employees set out the chairs and tables for business. They talked until noon, until he remembered he had to take a friend to pick up his car at the repair shop. When he said goodbye, he leaned over and cupped her head in both his hands, then kissed her on the lips. He remembers how each of them held that kiss, not opening their mouths, but not pulling away either. He remembers the fullness of her lips against his, how he knew in that moment he was home. And he remembers how when he finally pulled away and opened his eyes, the smile that greeted him was the most beautiful he'd ever seen.

He thinks he feels the corners of his mouth tilting up the slightest bit. He keeps himself from looking in the mirror, afraid he won't be able to bear another disappointment, but then he's so sure that something like happiness is moving through him. The same feeling he almost felt that time when a previous version of himself brought home a puppy. That experiment had almost worked until the puppy got sick all over the new carpet. But this is different, isn't it? He's nearly sure he feels a warmth spreading from his center. Yes! Yes! This is it! He raises his gaze, but the same straight carrot face looks back. Isn't that what they'd called him all those years ago in that movie. He should have never taken the role. It seemed like such a good idea at the time, but as soon as that reporter had called him an "intellectual carrot" he knew it was a bad career move. He'd be typecast, doomed to playing the same role over and over. And how many roles are there in Hollywood for walking carrots anyway?

Oh what a prophetic man Doctor Carrington turned out to be! What did it matter that he was a character in a horror movie nearly thirty years ago? "The perfect being," he'd said. "No pain or pleasure. No emotions. No heart. Far superior in every way." He got that right. Only it's not a blessing, it's a curse.

Jim calmly puts the umbrella back in its stand and

retires to the bedroom where he sleeps until noon. He can scarcely bring himself to rise in time for rehearsal. Some days he can't get out of bed. On those days, he's convinced he's at least able to feel the numbness of depression as he curls into a fetal position and pulls the covers about him. He's been fired from a few jobs over the years for not showing up, which is why he now makes a pittance working community theatre in a suburb of Denver. They normally don't pay their actors at all, but they're so thrilled to get a one time "star," they actually give him standard SAG rates, hoping they'll make up for it with concessions.

He rises from bed and walks to the window, peering out over his backyard garden. The midday sun usually gives him enough energy to commit himself to another day. He bathes in the warmth, but today it does nothing for him. Maybe he won't go in. Maybe today will mark the end of his acting career. Maybe he'll stay in his room until a passerby smells the rotting corpse and ventures inside only to find him gone soft, his skin wrinkled and gray, shoots sprouting from his body.

A breeze blows through the open window, and he swears he hears a ringing. Faint, but there nonetheless. It can't be. She used to ring it in the morning to wake him, to make sure he didn't go back to sleep. He stills his heart, something that's not too difficult as his heart beats at a fraction of the speed of a human one. He closes his eyes, feels the breeze on his face. There it is again! A sound smaller than rain. Waking him to himself. He goes to his bedside table, opens the drawer. A tiny bell sits atop the collected poems of Rumi. He reaches for it, but stops. The sound was a trick of his imagination, nothing more.

Nikki had left him over a year ago. How many versions of himself had he grown and burned since then? Too many to count. He needs to have his ears checked. He is a rational being. A creature of the highest intellect. The descendent of an alien race capable of space flight before humans were walking upright. He put that bell in the drawer for a reason, never wanting to see it again because it reminded him of what he wasn't, what he could never be. He should have thrown it away. He needed to let go if he was going to move forward in his life.

Who was he kidding? He couldn't be more stuck. Before Nikki, he'd never had the need to grow a new self, to burn the old one. Now, it was an addiction. A way of coping with the fact that he'd lost the woman he would have loved had he only had the ability to love. Each day waking and wondering if he would be different. Each day, staring into the bathroom mirror and seeing the same old self. He punches a hole in the window screen, then grabs the bell. He raises his fist, ready to throw the bell into his neighbor's yard when he swears he hears the ringing sound again. There must be something wrong with him. He really should see a doctor. Superior being or not, he needs medical attention. But then again, why bother. He'll only be around for the day and then the new Jim will take his place. Let the new Thing worry about a possible brain tumor.

He looks out at the garden, where he'd been growing only six hours before. He can still see the tendril of root that once attached to his ankle. If he closed his eyes and inhaled, he could still smell the dirt in his pores. He needs to shower before work. But why should he do anything at all? Why do anything outside of the ridiculous pattern his life has fallen into? Wake at noon. Live twelve hours hoping somehow this version will be the one who actually feels. Then burn yourself to cinders wondering, as the flames lick your body, if perhaps this next one will finally understand who you are.

That's the last thing Nikki said to him: *Who are you?* Almost two years together, and she still didn't know him. They sat across each other in the Sushi Den, the waiter having just brought the Saki. They hadn't even ordered yet, and she looked him in the eye and said those three words. He'd actually bought a ring. He kept it in his pocket, waiting for the right moment, thinking after the Miso soup and before the California rolls would be the right time. But that time never came. He couldn't answer her. Oh, he tried, mumbling something about vegetable matter not needing to bother itself with petty things like identity and feelings, but she wouldn't leave it alone. *You don't let me in,* she'd said. And he remembered wondering if there was anything inside to let her into. He left her alone just as they started up the karaoke machine. He vowed he wouldn't speak to her again until he could grow a new self, one that could offer something inside, something she could know.

He sets the bell on the windowsill where its gold surface catches the light, nearly blinding him. He closes his eyes and stares at the orange spots, waiting for them to assemble into a sign, anything that will tell him what to do. Now I've really gone over the deep end, he thinks. That's it! Let it burn. Let it burn holes in my retina so I can't see. He opens his eyes and stares directly into the reflected light, but after a few seconds he has to turn away. Over a year, and I'm no closer, he thinks. Over three hundred and sixty-five new versions of me, and nothing's changed. He cups the bell in his hand and kisses it, then puts it back in the drawer. "I'm done running," he says to himself. "One way or another, it ends with me." He walks out back, takes the hoe from the shed and tears up the garden, knocking out the remaining roots and chopping them into little pieces. He douses the pieces with gasoline and sets a match to them. When nothing remains, he spreads the ashes, digging up the ground beneath to make sure no roots remain that might take hold.

Inside, he hunts down his sunglasses and car keys with renewed purpose. Yes, perhaps this is the answer after all. To take a stand. To walk through the fire and out the other side. And so, he scarcely hears the shouts of the protestors who've been camped out in front of his house for as long as he can remember. As he backs out of the garage, he pays no notice to the signs saying: "We Don't Need Calculating Carrots!" or "Take your Superior Vegetable Matter Back to Outer Space!" or "If God Intended Vegetables to Think, He Wouldn't Have Made Tomatoes Taste So Good!" The idiots! Didn't they understand that tomatoes weren't even vegetables? When the Vegans first started coming to his door, shouting obscenities in his face, he'd simply kill them. How else could he maintain the blood surplus needed to grow his new selves? Killing them was easy as they usually appeared alone or at most in pairs. Never the "rule of four." Funny how stupid humans can be, especially when they're juiced up for a cause. And the Vegans couldn't be more upset. They'd thought they understood things, that they had the superior moral ground, eating life that wasn't sentient. So they weren't too happy when the news spread about a walking carrot, especially one who could build spaceships out of spare auto parts.

He smiles and waves to them as he backs down the driveway, which just incites them more. They yell and curse at him, chanting: "Take Back our Veggies!" and "Hit the Street. We won't go back to meat!" as they lie down head to toe, blocking his path to the theatre. He could run them over. Teach them to stay out of his way. But he is tired of violence. The blood would only remind him of his old life, the need to grow a new self, and he wants no more of that. There must be another way. He stops the car and steps out.

"Listen," he says. "Can't we all just get along?"

"No!" the Vegans scream, covering their eyes and ears. "Stop it! Vegetables can't talk!" Two of the Vegans stand and consider making a run for it.

"I don't want to hurt you," Jim says, stepping toward them again, palms out in a gesture of peace.

"Don't come any closer," the Vegans scream. "You can't walk! It's impossible!"

"Other plants walk," Jim replies. "What about the walking cactus or wandering vines?"

"That's not real walking!" screams the young man who has been their leader for the past two months, at least since Jim pulled the limbs from the other one.

"It's still movement," Jim explains, raising his arms in frustration.

A few more Vegans jump away, breaking their line. "Hold firm!" their leader shouts, but even he looks as if he's going to wet his pants.

Jim steps forward. The remaining Vegans scatter. The

leader yells to remain calm, even as he lies on the road, eyes squeezed shut. Jim kneels beside him. "Get away!" the leader shouts. But Jim reaches out, attempting to take the leader's hand in his own. The leader crawls backward like a crab, and the rest of the Vegans follow. Problem solved. Jim wishes he would have thought of the peaceful path before. He gets back in his car and drives off.

Each time he steps into the theatre, he swears he sees Nikki. Sometimes it's just the swish of her dress disappearing around a corner. Other times, her smile flashes before him the moment he opens the door. It doesn't help that playbills line the hallway, covered with pictures of her. He's trained himself to avoid the posters, to look straight ahead as he walks, but her face haunts him just the same.

The theatre is a buzz as they've just posted the cast list for the new production. Everyone's been excited to do *The Fantastiks* since they'd announced the schedule last spring. He passes Bob in the box office with a brisk hello, then makes his way down the hall to the auditorium where they post the parts. He doesn't know which he'd rather be: El Gallo or Matt. Both parts have equal billing. Both offer him chances to push his abilities. If Nikki hadn't left the company, he would have refused the part of Matt. Playing the romantic lead opposite her would have been too much. Now he's ready for whatever fate throws his way.

Ken and Doug appear at the other end of the hall, but they pretend not to see him and double back the way they came. That's odd. They've been friends for as long as he's been a part of the company. Three years now. In fact, they've always been the first to congratulate him when he lands a new lead. Maybe, they didn't get the parts they wanted. Poor sods! He better give them time to recover. He continues on, passing the bathroom just as Paul emerges drying his hands with a paper towel.

"Have you seen the list yet?" Jim asks. "What will I be singing "Try to Remember" or "Soon it's Gonna Rain?"

Paul dabs his forehead with the paper towel, avoiding eye contact. "Haven't had a chance to see it yet, Jim," he replies. "But you probably shouldn't expect to get the lead every time." He gives a nervous laugh, then tries to escape.

"That's funny," Jim says, taking his arm. "You're funny. But remember, I'm the star. The one people pay to see." He gives Paul his best movie poster smile. "Am I right?"

"It's 1983," Paul mumbles. "Time marches on." He steps out of Jim's grasp and shuffles sheepishly around the corner.

How could anyone forget? *Time* magazine had named *The Thing from Another World* the greatest monster movie of the fifties. They would do good to remember that. Maybe his time here was up. Maybe leaving the company was another step in the journey he'd started this morning. They were small time. He was meant for bigger things. No. He was getting ahead of himself. One step at a time. It's never good to make too many changes in one day. And he loved *The Fantastiks*. He'd been begging them to do it since he joined.

At last, he reaches the stage door. Dewey runs his finger down the cast list. He's always had a soft spot for Dewey, a short, pudgy character actor past his prime.

Dewey takes whatever part he's given and rolls with it. Jim knows there is a lesson in there for him somewhere if he can only see it.

"Don't tell me," Jim says, placing a hand on Dewey's shoulder. "You got the part of Bellamy."

"You guessed it," Dewey replies "Another doddery old father for me."

"And what will it be for me?" Jim asks.

Dewey blanches. "I thought you'd heard," he says. "I mean..."

"No one tells me anything around here," Jim jokes. "You know the star is always the last to know."

"Nikki's back," Dewey says, his eyes shifting down the corridor as if she might suddenly appear. "She's playing the female lead."

Jim steadies himself against the exposed brick wall. "What are you talking about?"

"You know the company hasn't been the same since she left." Dewey slowly backs down the hallway as he talks. "Management wanted her back. They hoped you'd understand."

"Of course," Jim says. He braces himself against the wall now with both hands.

"You don't look well." Dewey stops at the end of the hall.

"It's nothing," Jim replies. "I had some orange juice earlier, and it upset my stomach, that's all."

"Good. We were worried, you know. Given your past history with Nikki."

Jim waves the comment away and almost slips down the wall. "I'm a professional. Whatever's good for the company. And besides I'm beyond all that now. I'm happy to play El Gallo if it will help. I kind of hoped for that part in fact."

"Well, I'm late to take my daughters to piano lessons," Dewey says. "I'll catch you later." And before Jim can say another word, Dewey disappears around the corner.

Jim scans the cast list. The part of Matt will be played by someone named John. They haven't had a John in the company. Must be a new actor. Well that's better. It's important to have new blood. He couldn't stand the thought of any of the other cast members kissing Nikki anyway. El Gallo was really the lead. A much better turn for him. El Gallo was no simple romantic lead, like the part of Matt. It demanded versatility. Fate was already lending a hand. He would pour all his frustrated energy into the part, showing Nikki what she was missing and staging his comeback all at the same time.

He read further down the list. El Gallo will also be played by someone named John. There must be some mistake. Could it be a typo? They meant to type Jim, but it somehow came out as John. Even as he thinks this he knows it can't be true. Mistyping one letter is certainly possible but three letters. It's no typo. Still, two new Johns in the company would be strange. And no one informed him of any new hires. Something's wrong. He scans the rest of the cast list. Sure enough. Nikki really is playing Luisa. He says her name out loud without realizing it, then catches himself. *Nikki.* He looks around, afraid someone heard him. He sees her face, dark eyes that write themselves on his own. He feels her lips pressed to his. No. Today is the day he moves forward with his life. Not back. The new Jim is going to focus on his career. The new Jim wants to be back in the limelight. So, what part did he get? He'll show them he's happy to take anything. He scans the list again. Maybe they're giving him a rest. It was an awful strain playing Macbeth in the last production. They must have seen the way he carried the part home with him and wanted to give him a break. That's it. They've always looked after his wellbeing. He should have known better. But then he catches his name on the last line of the cast list. "The Wall!" he shouts.

He doesn't even knock before entering the artistic director's office. Ed sits behind his desk, his head buried in a small book, but he closes it quickly and stands when Jim enters, extending a stiff hand.

"Don't play nice with me, Ed!" Jim slaps his hand out of the way. "The Wall! Really? Did you think I'd take that lying down?"

Ed opens his mouth, starts to speak, but Jim continues on.

"Damn it, Ed, I'm the star of this company. That's why you brought me in here. I've been the lead in every production going on three years. What are you doing casting me as The Wall?"

Ed opens his desk drawer and pulls out a copy of *The Denver Post*. He points to an article circled in red. "Do you remember this?" he asks.

"I don't read reviews," Jim replies. "No artist worth his salt reads reviews."

"They said your Macbeth was stiff."

Jim tears the paper from his hand and reads it over. "How many times do I have to tell people? I was playing him as cut off from his emotions. His inner child had been crushed! Besides what the hell do critics know?"

"All I know is when you get a review like this," Ed

goes on. "It's bad for business."

"So you hired two actors named John." Jim tosses the paper back at Ed. "You couldn't leave me with El Gallo."

"What are you talking about?" Ed replies. "We only hired one John. We could barely afford him as it was, coming off his recent success. But for some reason he seems willing to slum it. His agent says he wants to shed the Hollywood image and get in touch with his theatrical roots." He carefully folds the paper and puts it back in his desk. He pulls out another paper with yet another article highlighted, but this time he reads the headline to Jim: "The secret to Carpenter's *The Thing* is the creature itself. To put it bluntly, move over Brando, this Thing can act!"

Jim sits down and scratches his head. "They remade my movie?" he asks absently.

"Yep," Ed says.

"And you hired this new "star" to play both leads in our production?"

"He's one hell of an actor."

"John?"

"Yes, John."

"And now I'm playing The Wall?"

"Yep."

"And this all makes perfect sense to you?"

Ed leans in close, whispering to Jim for effect. "We thought the part would play to your strengths."

Jim doesn't remember leaving Ed's office. He doesn't remember walking down the corridors of the theatre, mumbling to himself something about "the superior race of vegetables." He's not sure how he drove home since he has no memory of that either, the only evidence being the Vegan he squashed in the entrance to his driveway.

It is not until he finds himself leaning over the bath, the knife held so tight against his middle finger he actually draws a drop of juice, that he regains his senses. He takes the knife to the garden and buries it where he would have buried his own finger, his hands shaking as he does so. He tries to catch his breath but the harder he tries, the more difficult it is to breathe. Soon, he is hyperventilating. He lies down in the dirt. Breathe, he tells himself. Breathe. You are a professional. This is just a little set back. Remember, what matters is how you walk through the fire. That's right. You are not walking out on this production. You're not going to let Nikki see you quit. She's not going to watch you cave to some one-hit wonder so sure of himself he wants two parts! And then it hits him. She's back. Nikki is back in his life. He has a second chance. This is exactly what he needs. To show her that he is capable of changing. If she sees him handling a minor role with aplomb, what else might she think he's capable of? Feeling. Why not? He'll be the most emotive Wall the theatre has ever seen! Love! Of course! The wall is a symbol for the obstacles all great love must face! He'll show her he can break through that wall. Yes, he tells himself. This is the part you've been waiting for! There's just one problem. She'll have to kiss John. She'll have to act as if she loves him. And what if John slips her the tongue? What if he tries something worse? He needs to know who this so-called actor is. He needs to know his strengths and more importantly, his weaknesses.

He gets back in his car, slaloming through the Vegans as he makes his way to the video store. It's easy to find a copy. In fact, there's a whole wall of them. John

Carpenter's *The Thing*. He's never heard of this director. What did he know of making horror movies? The idiot had to rely on making a remake. Probably another hack Hollywood hired to save a buck. Back home, two hours later, he sits on his couch in shock. Apart from the first thirty minutes where the audience wonders what's the matter with the mysterious dog that arrives at the arctic camp, the film was disgusting. No real character development. No meticulous creation of fear through atmosphere. Just gore. Special effect piled on special effect. Heads growing legs and walking around like spiders. Teeth appearing in chests and chomping off arms. It didn't even make sense! Why would the Thing enter one body only to obliterate that body a few scenes later? He wasn't even a vegetable any more! The damn director changed his whole persona. This new Thing was a shapeshifter, a doppelganger, able to become whatever he came in contact with. This new Thing was a fraud! There was no real acting involved here. The special effects took care of everything. All this idiot had to do was roll around shaking on the floor while tentacles shot out of him grabbing on to anything that moved! Where was the deep yearning, the inner conflict he'd so clearly conveyed that gave the original such poignancy? Where was the angst, the despair, at being alone in the world, cut off from your own kind? No. This new Thing was nothing more than a trick of the camera, a special effect without heart. He couldn't act his way out of a box. He was no threat. Nikki would be his before they finished the staged readings. He slept better that night than he had in a long time.

The next day, he makes sure to be the last to arrive

at rehearsal, walking in a half hour late wearing his Ray Bans. They're already in the middle of blocking the scene where the lovers meet at the wall, but they're using a chair for his part. He isn't prepared for the beauty of Nikki's back. The black hair falling on that smooth, olive skin. He loved kissing her neck, her shoulders. He can't help but notice where those shoulders meet the white cotton dress. It's the same one she wore the night they first met. She had to have known that, to have worn it for a reason. He follows the contour of the dress down her slim frame. She's not wearing any shoes. He's always loved her feet. They do something to him he can't explain. Suddenly, he can't breathe. He's afraid he'll hyperventilate again.

"Nice of you to show," Ed calls over his shoulder.

Nikki turns to him, but he pretends to notice his shoe needs tying.

"Spent the morning preparing, looking over my lines," Jim says, as he gives his shoes double knots.

"You don't have any lines!" Ed replies, then signals for the others to break their tableau. "Listen, I want to get this production started on the right foot. Are you with me?"

"Why do you think I'm tying my shoes?" he replies, finally looking up, thankful the Ray Bans offer some protection.

"Let's start over," Ed says. "I don't believe you and John have met."

John flashes a broad smile and sticks out his hand. "You have some tough shoes to fill, Big Guy," he says. "I hope I'm up for it."

Jim steps forward, takes his hand firmly. "I hope so, too." Each attempts to stare down the other. Blue bedroom eyes. Five O'clock shadow. He must think he's the cat's meow, Jim thinks. Ed shouts for them to take it from the top.

"This is your heroic moment," Ed tells John. "The whole song is a metaphor for how you love her in the grandest way possible."

"Got it," John replies as he steps up on the chair. "I think it would be good to deliver it from here, over the wall."

"Great idea." Ed gestures Jim into position. "I'd like you to stand between them, bend your head over onto your right shoulder and stick your arm out like this."

"Excellent. I'm channeling the wall already," Jim replies, getting into position facing away from Nikki and toward John. I'll be the best damn wall anyone's ever seen, he thinks.

Ed gives the signal to John to begin his song. "Remember what I said. You love her as no one has ever loved."

John extends his arms to the heavens and belts out the tune. *I don't know what to call her. She is too vibrant for a name. Should I call her, Juliet?*

Yes, dear! Nikki sings back.

Suddenly, Jim's knees go wobbly. Oh God! Her voice. He wasn't prepared for her voice at all. He feels faint. The room is getting darker. I need to take off these Ray Bans, he thinks.

Helena!

Yes, dear!

And Cassandra, and Cleopatra, and Beatrice, and also. . .

"Hold it! Hold it!" Ed cries out, waving his arms for

them to stop. "Jim, your wall is sagging."

"It wasn't sagging," Jim replies from his hunched position.

"It was definitely sagging," John adds, stepping off his chair. "You're practically on your knees."

"How can I not sag?" Jim stands, looking from Ed to John. He doesn't dare steal a glance at Nikki. "He's got the part of Matt all wrong," Jim replies, standing on his chair to make his point. "He's embellishing too much. It's overblown. It should be more subdued, more contained."

"Oh Christ!" Ed says. "Everyone take a break."

Jim can hear Nikki's groan as she walks away. "I'm serious," he says. "There is a world of love burning inside him if he'll only let it out. But he can't. He doesn't know how. That's the heart of Matt's character!"

"Why don't you let me play the part," John says, stepping up on the chair.

"Hey, you're crowding me here," Jim replies.

"I'm Matt. You're The Wall. You get it." John pokes his finger into Jim's chest, threatening to knock him off the chair.

"You're also El Gallo," Jim replies, grabbing the finger in his fist and holding it. "Don't you think two leads is a bit much for a guy whose only acting experience involves rolling around on the floor while tentacles and teeth shoot out of him?"

"Why you son-of-a. . ." John raises his fist.

"Gentleman," Ed breaks in, wedging his hands between them, pushing them both off the chair. "You are professionals. Start behaving that way."

"This guy's nothing but an impostor," Jim says. "Have

you seen the remake? It's embarrassing. He doesn't have to emote or feel anything!"

"Are you sure you're not talking about yourself," Nikki offers from the doorway. They are the first words she's addressed to him in over a year. But when he hears them it's as if time collapses, and he's with her again. It doesn't matter what she's saying. She could tell him she hates his guts, and he'd still want to hear that voice.

Jim takes off his Ray Bans and steps toward her. He's going to tell her to forget the past, tell her they have a chance to start over right here. Right now. But she shoots him the same look she did that night in the Sushi Den. The look that says she no longer believes what he has to say. He can't handle that. Anything but that. He freezes up, not able to say a thing. She walks out the door.

"You've finally got your part down," John says, patting him on the back. "Not a word. That's The Wall." He exits quickly behind Nikki. .

"We don't even know who this guy is," Jim pleads with Ed. "I mean what kind of movie was he in, anyway? They changed the whole story! It's not a remake. The Thing is not supposed to be some sort of human chameleon, taking on a new identity whenever it suits him. He is a walking carrot!"

"Shut up, Jim," Ed says, throwing his hands in the air. He grabs his coffee cup, his script.

"Do you even know who you've hired here?" Jim asks. "He's not the real Thing, I'm telling you! He's a fraud!" Jim screams as Ed slams the door.

Jim looks around the empty room. I'm alone, he thinks. I'm a freak. Nikki doesn't want anything to do with me. "Nikki," he whispers. "Nikki!" he shouts louder.

"Not Juliet. Not Helena. Not Cassandra. Not Cleopatra. Not even Guinevere." He runs out the door and into the parking lot where she's just about to get into her car. "Stop!" he shouts.

She turns to him. Even now she looks so tall, so regal. A strong woman. The only woman for him. And for a moment he thinks he sees a tinge of hope on her face. But then she speaks. "Haven't you done enough already?"

He stops a few feet before her. Better to give her some distance. Don't make her feel pushed. But when he tries to speak, he realizes the run to the parking lot winded him more than he thought.

"Well, say what you came to say," she says, anger now masking whatever it was he saw in her face. She always did anger easily. He used to say that was part of their strength as a couple. Because he had no emotions her anger couldn't hurt him.

"You are not Juliet!" he finally manages to say.

"Well, thank you for sharing." She opens her car door. "Is that what you came running and screaming over here for?" She looks disappointed. He's sure of it. She has hope. Somewhere beneath the hurt, there's hope.

"What I mean to say is that I'm not putting you on a pedestal," he continues.

"I think I've heard enough." She gets in the car and closes the door. Luckily she's left the window open. He runs over and sticks his hand inside to keep her from rolling it up.

"I may not be able to feel," he goes on. "I may not be able to love, but at least it's not some romantic illusion. I can promise you truth."

She rolls up her window anyway.

"See, you can't hurt me. Isn't that worth something?" He is sure he sees something in her eyes. Love? Pity?

"Let me go," she says. "Or I'll scream."

"Look what passion brought those other women," he says. "Juliet. Guinevere. Cassandra. Nothing but pain and death. Am I right?"

"Yes, you're right," Nikki replies, her face stone. "Now can I go?" She starts the engine.

"Isn't it better to be with someone who can't feel? Someone who is comfortable? No need to risk all that pain, right?"

She rolls down the window, and for a moment Jim thinks he's gotten through to her. "I knew it," he says. "I knew you'd come . . ."

"You're the fraud, Jim," Nikki cuts him off. "For a time I thought maybe you could love. But I was wrong. I see now it was all an act. And not a very good one. You can't even act, Jim. And I fell for it. I almost really fell for it." Her voice breaks at the last. She turns away

"Nikki, please don't..."

"You're the fraud," she says again, staring straight ahead, as if she doesn't dare look at him. She drives off, nearly taking Jim's arm with her.

"I wish you had torn off my arm," he shouts after her. "Then you could grow a new me!"

He walks out of the parking lot and down the street, unaware of where he's going. Maybe she's right, he thinks. Maybe I am the fraud. I'll bet that bastard Hawks made me up for the movie. I'll bet he invented the whole idea of a walking carrot, and John's the real Thing. Who's afraid of a giant vegetable, anyway? You can't even love a vegetable because a vegetable can't love. But John. Well, he's different. You want a Romeo? He can become that. You want Bogart from *The Big Sleep.* Easy. You want Brando from *On the Waterfront,* he can become that, too. He wanders down tenth, then Sycamore until he stumbles into the community garden the Vegans keep. "Get away from here!" they shout. "You don't belong here!" He stumbles past, shoving them aside if they get too close. Then he stops and sits among the carrots and green beans. "You're right. I don't belong here," he whispers to himself. "I'm nothing but a Hollywood invention. Not even an interesting one. What would Nikki ever see in me, anyway? An actor who can't feel. It's like some sort of bad joke." He grabs a spade from a passing Vegan. "Hey, what the hell . . ." the Vegan starts to protest before Jim swats him away. He spends the rest of the afternoon digging a hole for himself.

By the time he has finished, only his head is above ground, staring at a crowd of Vegans who've gathered. They nod their approval, then water him before dispersing into the evening. He is thankful he's facing west. The sunset over the mountains bleeds reds and purples. Perhaps it will ignite him. Maybe fate has found a way to continue his cycle of immolation and rebirth. Anything is better than this. This in between place. This place somewhere between life and death. For as long as he can remember, he has wished he was leading a different life. He has wished to be a different person. And now this thing who calls himself an actor comes along able to be any person he wants to be. He can take on their appearance, their character, even their feelings. It simply isn't fair. Better to take root and stop trying. He closes his eyes and waits for darkness.

The sound of a bell echoes through his dream. He sees her through the window of the café where they talked that first morning together. She is sitting on a stool facing him. She smiles when she sees him. He walks in the door sure of himself, but as soon as she rises to move toward him, he collapses. At first he doesn't know why his face is so wet. He wipes away the tears as he kneels on the floor. The other patrons seem to ignore him. She stands over him, reaching out her hand. He tries to take it, but he cannot because the tears keep coming. If he doesn't stop them, if he doesn't wipe them away, he'll break in two. He's sure of it. So, he rubs the heels of both hands in his eyes to try and stem the tide. She opens her mouth to speak to him, but instead of her voice he hears bells, tiny little bells that sound like snowflakes. Again, he tries to take her hand, but now the water from his tears rises about him, and he has to fight to stay afloat. He swims about the café, looking for her, and still the tears keep coming. The water rises and rises, until all he can do is press his mouth against the roof of the café, gasping for every last bit of air.

"What are you doing here?" she asks, breaking his dream.

He opens his eyes and sees her beautiful, bare feet before him, the anklet of tiny bells glistening in the moonlight.

"You know how much the Vegans hate you," she goes on. "This is a dangerous place."

Her voice enters him like a swooping sparrow. "I don't care anymore," Jim replies, spitting out a mouth full of dirt. "I'm a fraud, remember."

She kneels down before him. "You know for someone

who supposedly can't feel emotion, you seem to find it pretty easy to tap into a well of self pity."

"Very funny," he says. The last few bits of dirt cling to his lips.

"Here, let me clean you." She wipes the dirt away. He swears her hand lingers there longer than it needs to.

"I really care for you," he says. Her eyes look even darker at night. Fertile soil for his soul.

"Shut up," she replies. "Don't even start with that. I don't want to hear it."

"And we were comfortable together," he continues.

"Don't!"

"And the sex was pretty good."

She picks up a handful of dirt and throws it in his face. "Shut up!"

He spits the dirt out once again, a line of drool running down his chin. "I can't see!"

"I'm sorry," she says. And again, she tries to clean him off. She starts out roughly, but her last few strokes soften.

"Isn't that love?" he asks as she wipes her hands off on her dress.

"No, it's not."

The way she looks at him now. Her eyebrows arching. Her eyes losing focus, as if she sees past him. Leaning forward. Her lips blooming. He is sure she feels something for him still. And he knows he wants to be with her. That's all he's ever wanted for the last year. It's what drove him to destroy and remake himself over and over. Wasn't that love? To want to be with someone? To share the same space with them? "Nikki?"

"Yes."

"The sex was good, wasn't it?"

She looks at him as if he's an idiot. "It was okay."

"That was a fraud, too?"

She gives him a sympathetic smile.

"Why are you here now, cleaning me off?"

"Because you're an asshole." She stands, looking down at him. "I'm here for the good of the troupe, nothing more."

"Did Ed send you?"

"No," she replies. "The company is only as good as its weakest link."

"Now you're saying I'm weak?"

"No, only that we need you."

"We need me or you need me?"

"We."

She gets that look in her face again. He's sure of it. Her brow furrows when she's hiding something. There's still a chance. "Where do we go from here, Nikki?"

She doesn't miss a beat. "Nowhere."

It's as if the dirt rises around him. He chokes, coughing horribly. She starts to kneel, as if she might clean him off again, but then she stops. "No," she whispers, so softly he wonders if he imagined it. "No, I won't." She turns from him and walks away. He wants to shout out for her to wait. He wants to tell her that she's the one who doesn't know how to love. How could she walk away from a man fighting for breath. She's the one who doesn't feel anything.

An earthworm rises out of the ground and inches along in front of his mouth. He hopes there aren't any other creepy crawlies eating away at his body beneath the earth. That's the last thing he needs right now. The problem is he doesn't know what he needs. He came here to end it. He let the Vegans bury him. And now, she walks into his life and tells him there's nowhere left for them to go. That's what he'd wanted, right? He didn't want to go anywhere at all, except to be food for worms. Everything should be okay. But it wasn't. How could she cut him out like that so completely? It didn't make any sense. Why have feelings if you could shut them off when things got too painful? Maybe he was of a superior race after all. He didn't have to cut off his emotions when it got too painful because he didn't feel pain. He could endure bucket loads of pain. So, why was he buried up to his neck in the dirt? He should be out courting pain. He should be showing them he could handle anything. He could play The Wall if that's what they wanted. He could still work alongside the woman who left him. The next time they questioned his abilities, they'd remember how strong he really was. How he put them all to shame when it came to enduring pain! And that's what he's thinking when the sun rises and two young boys with buckets and little shovels sit down next to him to make a dirt castle. They want to use his head as a turret.

"Do you think you could dig me out?" he asks.

"If you pay us two dollars," the smaller boy says.

"Fine. Fine. Just do it quickly."

With their little shovels it takes them most of the morning. Still, he's able to make it to rehearsal, dirt staining his white button up.

He arrives late only to find Nikki sitting on the couch with John, killing time with small talk. Ed is pacing frantically, complaining about how Dewey hasn't shown up yet, which is strange because Dewey has always been the consummate professional. In fact, he hasn't missed a

91

rehearsal in twelve years. They were going to rehearse the song where the fathers complain about how they don't understand their children: *Plant a radish, get a radish not a Brussels sprout. That's why I love vegetables, you know what they're about.* Jim always loved that song. It was actually the main reason he'd pushed Ed to get the rights for the play in the first place.

"We're not wasting more time." Ed signals the actors to gather round. "We'll rehearse *Soon it's Going to Rain,* then we'll go straight into the abduction scene.

Is it Jim's imagination or does Nikki actually lean into John as they rise from the couch. Yes, she definitely leans into him! And look how she invades his space as they wait for instructions.

"Okay, John and Nikki, remember what it felt like to be in love for the first time. That's what this scene is all about. Draw on those memories." Ed moves about the room blocking the scene, showing how the lovers will walk through the forest as John sings to Nikki. "And Jim, you'll be the tree where they stop and kiss."

"I can be the whole forest," Jim says, moving into position. "Just watch." He spreads his arms and his legs trying to convey a forest but ends up pretzling them until he looks more like a game of *Twister.* "I think I've got it," he says.

"I'd rather you simply be one tree." Ed takes Jim's leg and untangles it from the other. "Let the audience use their imagination."

"Right, that's what theatre is all about," Jim says, snapping back into tree position.

Ed gives the cue to begin. "Hit it people."

John takes Nikki by the hand and leads her through

the forest, singing: *Hear how the wind begins to whisper. See how the leaves go streaming by . . .* He twirls Nikki around, then pulls her to the tree.

They are standing to his right, but Jim can see Nikki's face through the corner of his eye, and he doesn't like what he sees. She's got the look he knows all too well. The same look she had on her face the night she told him he was her first love as they sat on a bench in the garden at City Park, the sun setting over the Rockies. It had been the perfect end to a perfect date. Dinner. Dancing. A walk through the park under the moonlight. Is she drawing from memory for her acting or is this look the real thing? He isn't sure he likes either option, though the former is certainly the more palatable.

Now is the time to find a hide away, where we can stay. John takes her into his arms and continues singing. Jim can barely see her now, but he swears she's leaning into John again, her lips opening, inviting a kiss, even though there's no kiss in the script.

"Really," he says, dropping his tree pose. "That's looking like you're in love?"

Ed throws his script in the air. "What the hell are you doing, Jim?"

"She looks like she's got cancer, not like she's in love," Jim continues. Something in him knows this is a mistake, but he can't stop himself.

"Great!" Nikki says, hands on hips. "Cancer! That's really great!"

Jim tries to salvage the situation, taking Nikki by the arm, pulling him to her.

"Hey, what are you doing?" She fights him, but Jim holds her firm.

93

"I don't blame her," Jim says. "It would be tough for anyone to pretend they're in love with this guy, but here's how you do it." He puts on his most lovelorn face, the one every previous version of himself had practiced each day for the last year in front of the mirror: lower lip pouting, eyes drooping, all topped with a lover's sigh. Nikki screams and pulls her hand away, pointing at the front of Jim's shirt. An earthworm works its way up from the breast pocket to his shoulder. Jim plucks it from his shirt and sheepishly drops it out the open window.

"I think you've made your point," Ed says. "So, unless you have anything else to say, can we count on you to play the part you've been assigned without any more outbursts?"

Jim nods his head. "I promise from this time forth I will not speak again," he says.

"Thank you," Ed begins. "Now, can we . . ."

"I am a wall," Jim continues. "A mute wall. I will not speak until the play's run is over." They want method acting, they'll get method acting!

"Let's call it a day," Ed says, shaking his head. "Will somebody please contact Dewey and see what the hell is wrong." He exits, mumbling to himself.

"Thanks a lot," Nikki says. "Did you take pleasure in humiliating me like that? Oh wait, you can't take pleasure. In fact, you can't feel anything at all. I'm sorry."

I'm the one who's sorry, Jim wants to say, then realizes he's just vowed to be mute. Nikki gives him a moment, as if she's hoping for an apology, then takes John's arm and walks out. Jim can hear them as they walk down the hallway, John laughing about how her "ex" is quite the character. She actually laughs along with him before saying, "I don't know what I saw in him." Jim staggers to the couch. He closes his eyes and again sees her through the window of the café. "Give me a chance," he mouths to her, but she doesn't understand. He moves to the door, tries to open it, but it's jammed. He has to get inside. He must see her, hold her in his arms and tell her face to face how he feels. He grabs the handle with both hands and jerks the door open, but he is washed away in the flood of tears that gushes forth.

Jim wakes with a start, wiping the sweat from his face. He needs air. A walk in the park. Anything. He's got to clear his mind of Nikki. He makes his way down the hall but his throat is parched so he takes a short cut past the water cooler. That's when he notices the door to the janitor's closet is ajar, a broom handle sticking out of it at a slant. A bit untidy, he thinks and opens the door to put the broom away. The broom's brush sits in a puddle of blood. He steps back to take in the scene. Blood covers the floor, the walls. Everything. What the hell happened here? He sees the torn pages of someone's script scattered about the floor, some soaked in blood, others half-hidden behind the mop bucket and the bleach. He picks up a page, then another, trying to see whose script it is. Dewey's lines are highlighted in green.

He runs to Ed's office, throws open the door and holds the stained script pages aloft.

"Haven't you caused enough damage today already?" Ed says, looking up from his desk.

Jim opens his mouth to answer but remembers his vow of silence. How he would prove to them he could play the part of The Wall. How he would show them he was a better actor than the whole lot put together. He stands as if struck dumb.

"Well, what do you want?" Ed asks. "You barged in here for something."

Jim waves the paper back and forth in front of him as if he's signaling a taxi.

"I don't get it," Ed says. "What's going on?"

Jim panics. This is going to be harder than he thought. What can he do? He'll mime it, that's what! He was a mime on the streets of Barcelona one summer before he got his big break. He still knows what to do! He waddles around the office as if he's Dewey, brushing his thinning hair to the side, bowing when he meets someone as only Dewey can do. Once he feels he's established the character, he pretends he's getting a drink of water from the cooler when he's suddenly surprised. He backs away in terror.

"What in the hell are you doing?" Ed says, rising, arms raised in front of him, ready to push Jim from his office. "Have you lost your mind?"

Jim continues, now acting as if tentacles are shooting out of his midsection. He walks about with his best monster gait, pretending to take Dewey in a grip of death. He mimes undressing the corpse and putting the clothes on himself. For the coupe de grace, he pretends to be washing his hands of blood, tempted to recite Lady Macbeth as he does so.

"I hate to be the one to say this," Ed says when he's finished. "But you need a good, long vacation."

Jim can't believe it. He's sure he acted out the parts to perfection. Even a child could tell what was going on.

"When this play is over, I want you to take a break. Get some rest." Ed ushers him to the door.

Jim lets himself be pushed into the hallway. He's not even sure he understands what's going on himself. How could he explain it to Ed even if he chose to break from his method acting? He's starting to feel his hold on the world slipping. First Nikki tells him he's the fraud and now Dewey's been murdered, at least that's what it looks like. But he's beginning to lose faith in appearances.

He doesn't recognize his own house, as the Vegans are no longer camped out on the lawn, and so he drives past. In fact, he drives past twice before realizing what he is doing. Half a block down, he backs up and stares at his brick bungalow. It is his, isn't it? The events of the day have so disoriented him. For years, he'd defined himself by the daily antipathy of the Vegans. They'd become his lifeblood. Literally. And now even they've abandoned him. If anything else changes, he isn't sure he can go on. What he needs now is a stiff drink, he thinks. Maybe a little time to relax and gather himself. But when he opens the door to his home, he finds a dozen Vegans camped out in his living room. They made their own little shantytown and everything. At first, he's taken aback. The Vegans shout to one another to lie flat. "If he tries to pick you up, go limp," their leader says. Jim rushes in and hugs the leader before he can go limp himself.

"Thank you! Thank you," Jim says, forgetting his vow of silence.

"He's trying to squeeze me to death!" the leader shouts. "Help!"

"No," Jim says, though he still holds the leader in a bear hug. "I'm happy. I'm so happy. I wasn't sure who I was, but now you're here..." And then he catches himself. Did he just say he was happy? What does that mean? Is he smiling? He lets go of the leader and runs to the hall mirror. Nothing. He tries to find the feeling again, to analyze it, but it's gone.

"We're occupying your house in the name of animals everywhere," the leader begins his speech. "Your existence threatens little piggies, cows, chickens, ducks, lambs, even frogs and snakes. Go back to where you came from." The rest of the Vegans stand beside him and shout their agreement.

"But I crashed on your planet over one hundred thousand years ago," Jim replies, trying the same tired argument he's used before. "By every definition, I'm the original Native American."

"You're still a threat, and we're going to occupy this house until you leave." The Vegans link arms, making a human wall, then begin walking toward Jim, pushing him out the front door, chanting: "Hell no! We won't go!"

Jim offers no resistance. He's still thinking about the happiness he might have felt. Maybe it was just thankfulness. Are they the same? Does being thankful count as an emotion? He needs to talk with someone. But whom? He has no real friends. No one who cares for him. No one for whom he cares. Wait a second. He does. He does have someone.

He stands before Nikki's front door, hesitant. Is it fear he feels? He no longer trusts himself. Once the floodgates have opened, he might be capable of feeling anything, doing anything. But then he wonders if he is only hesitating because rationally he knows she won't be happy to see him. In fact, she might be quite angry. He needs a plan. Maybe his "thankfulness" was only the result of rationalization as well. He was concerned about his own sanity, unsure who he was, and the Vegans offered concrete evidence he was still a walking vegetable. He still had a place in the world as their adversary, as the superior being. He could have simply been confirming that place with the hug. Gratitude doesn't have to be tied to feeling. It's then the door opens, John and Nikki practically falling through it as they embrace, kissing each other. Jim stands for a long moment, then pretends he has something in his eye.

"What are you doing here?" Nikki says, pulling herself from John's arms.

"Uh ..." Jim stammers.

"What?" John asks, putting his arm around Nikki as if she were his property. "Oh, I forgot. You're the great method actor."

"We're going to the movies," Nikki says as she brushes past him.

"I don't suppose you want to join us?" John says, as if finishing her sentence. He pulls her to the car.

The guy is smart. Jim has to hand it to him. But he's not about to join them on a date. "Can we talk, Nikki? Something's happening to me..."

"The Wall wants to talk, would you look at that." John helps Nikki into the car. Nikki stares straight ahead.

"Don't be afraid of how you feel," Jim says as the door shuts. He is almost sure that Nikki glances back at him as they drive away.

He finds himself wandering City Park as dusk falls. He stops at the bench where she told him she loved him. Various couples have carved their initials into the back: "Wallace and Elizabeth forever," "Devon and Karen always." It's hard to see in the thin light as he uses his keys to carve, "Jim loves Nikki," and carving is harder than he thought. By the time he's done, it's too dark to see if it's legible. Still, he knows it's there, and that's what counts. It seems important to him somehow. Maybe writing it makes it true. Didn't he see one of those daytime talk shows once where a psychologist talked about re-programming your neural pathways to feel what you want. Of course, that implied you could feel. He lies on the bench repeating to himself *I love Nikki* until the night turns brisk, and he curls up and falls asleep.

He staggers into rehearsal the next day determined not to make a mess of things. If Nikki wants to be with someone else, that's her prerogative. He's going to work on himself. After all, you can't love someone if you're not whole, and he's starting to realize he has a lot of missing pieces.

Dewey, or at least someone who appears to be Dewey, is back, but Paul is now missing. They still can't rehearse the scene with the fathers. Nikki and John sit talking intimately on the couch as Ed paces the room. "We have three weeks before opening," he says, crossing in one direction. "God knows I try, but you can only work with what you have," he says, crossing the other direction. When Jim enters, Dewey greets him with his usual bow. He seems a bit stiff, Jim thinks. I wonder if he's sick. "We'll give it five more minutes, then to hell with it!" Ed shouts, stopping his pacing for a moment. Always insecure about their ability to memorize lines, Ken and Doug quiz each other over their parts, seemingly unaware that Ed is about to call off the whole thing. Jim tries to keep from watching Nikki, but can't help it. They've had sex, he knows it. You can see it in the way they sit beside each other, their bodies constantly touching as they talk. The distance broken between them. Jim stands uncomfortably until Dewey tries to make conversation.

"Ed sure is high strung," he says, patting Jim on the back.

Dewey has never patted him on the back before. He's sure of it. And that smile of his. It is Dewey's smile, but it's not. As if Dewey is trying to mimic his own smile in a mirror. Jim knows what that looks like all too well.

"What happened to you yesterday?" Jim asks, eyeing Dewey, letting him know he's onto him. "It's unlike you to miss rehearsal."

"Dentist appointment I'd forgotten about," Dewey replies, chuckling nervously. "It's funny how difficult it is to remember things the older you get."

"Especially, when we've had the rehearsal schedule set for months." Jim tries to mimic Dewey's smile, maybe he can push him a bit further.

It's then Ed calls it quits, saying if things don't improve by the next day he's cancelling the show. "And for God's sake," he adds. "Someone call Paul!"

"Things certainly are shaky," Dewey says to Jim. "I think it's best for all of us to go home and study our lines."

"Won't that be difficult without your script?" Jim asks.

"What do you mean?" Dewey's smile fades.

"I mean I found your script with blood on it," Jim continues.

"Oh that," Dewey replies, stepping away. "Yeah, I cut my finger. Terrible. You wouldn't believe the blood."

"Oh, I'd believe it." Jim's got him, he's sure of it.

"No big deal, though," Dewey says, walking backwards toward the door. "I'd memorized my lines already."

"You shouldn't have much studying to do then," Jim says, but Dewey is already bowing goodbye to everyone. Each bow stiffer than the last. Jim knows what he needs to do.

It's not that difficult for Jim to sneak into his own bedroom through the window. The hard part comes when he has to slither on the ground like a snake through several meditating Vegans. Still, he's almost home free. He eyes the VHS on the coffee table, but there is a plate of half-eaten baba ganoush sitting on top of it. His mistake is in trying to slide the tape out from under the baba ganoush in one quick movement. He knocks the plate over, and before he knows it, the Vegans have come out of their trance and piled on top of him. "Let's cut him up and eat him!" one of them shouts. "I've got some chili powder and olive oil," another says, already working to take off one of his shoes. "I've got cilantro and parsley," says another, as they wrestle him to a pinned position.

"Hypocrites!" Jim shouts. "Can't you see what you're doing?"

"We're going to have a feast, that's what we're doing," the leader says.

"But you're supposed to revere sentient life, not eat it!"

"You're nothing but a walking carrot," says the Vegan who now holds his shoe aloft.

He's always hated being called that. Even so, looking back, he's not sure it accounts for what happens next. It starts with an animal groan inside him. Like a cat in heat,

102

but deeper. The sound begins in his gut, spreading to his chest, and as it does so it carries a wave of pain that rocks his body until he shakes so violently the Vegans have to let go. "I am not a walking carrot!" he shouts. The pain twists and wrenches at his insides until he's no longer in control. "Look at me!" he says.

The Vegans stand in stunned silence.

He walks to the fireplace, picks up a handful of ashes and throws it into the air. "Do you see how I've yearned to be different?"

The leader shakes his head no.

"I wanted to be like you so badly, I killed myself every night." He takes another handful of ash and throws it at the Vegans. "This is all that's left of me!"

The leader kneels and picks up some of the ash.

"Do you hear me?" he says, throwing handful after handful of ash at them. "Do you hear what I'm saying? I am much more than a walking carrot!"

"Yes, we hear you," the leader says at last. The others repeat after him. "Yes, we hear you."

"God, I'm so sick of this!" he shouts. It's as if something pops in Jim's face. His jaw jerks. His brow bulges. His cheeks quiver. He can barely manage to get out the words before his face screws up in pain. "I am enough!"

"You can feel," the leader says.

"I can?" He starts to think, to analyze the feeling then stops himself.

The Vegans drop to their knees and genuflect before him.

Jim sounds his body. It's not the same, and he knows it. He can't deny it. The anxiety he's kept hidden in his gut. It's there. He understands what it is now. He's simply never acknowledged it before. And there's something else. A feeling similar to the one he gets after his espresso each morning. The feeling of being alive. Awake. A heightened sense of awareness. The fluttering of papers on the kitchen counter as the fan blows them. The deep greens from the pine outside the living room window. And what's that smell? Yes! That beautifully pungent smell of unwashed Vegans! It's all there for him. There is a world inside his body, too. A pulsing, pushing through him. If he has to name it, what would it be? Desire? The need to reach out and hug the next person he sees? To love and be loved? It could be, but there's more. Beneath all of it. Something he's kept hidden. A deep sense of . . . loneliness. Yes, that's it! The moment he names it, he knows it's true. He has felt alone for as long as he can remember. Those hundred thousand years frozen in the arctic ice were nothing compared to the loneliness he has felt once they thawed him out, the loneliness he feels now surrounded by people who don't understand him. No wonder he's shut off. Of course he hid his emotions, hid them so deep not even he could find them. How could he expect Nikki to love him when he had nothing to give her? He hasn't been authentic. He hasn't been real. Not ever. Not once since he stepped out of that ice block over thirty years ago and maybe even before that. He's kept his true self hidden away. But he wants to show her. Suddenly, he wants to show her more than anything. That's when the doorbell rings.

He runs to the door, sure that it's her, that somehow she heard him cry out. But it's only Ed.

"We've got to talk," he says, pushing his way into the entryway. "The show's in danger. I'm not convinced we can pull it off." Ed notices the Vegans prostrate on the floor. "Who are these people?" Then he thinks better of it. "Never mind. Best not to know the secret lives of actors."

"I'd like to help, Ed, but there's somewhere I have to be." Jim tries to move past him.

"You're the reason we're doing this show," Ed says, blocking his exit. "You're the one who said we're not a real community theatre until we do *The Fantastiks*." Ed takes him firmly by the arm.

Strange. Ed's never been a touchy person and certainly not one to use force. "Did you find Paul?" Jim asks.

"Yeah, yeah," Ed replies. "He's okay, he just had a dentist appointment."

"That's the same thing Dewey said."

"I guess it's that time of year. Anyway, he's not the problem."

"What's the problem?"

"You," Ed replies. "That's why I'm here." The Vegans begin chanting Jim's name. "Is there somewhere we can go that's private? I'd like to talk with you alone." Ed tries to pull Jim into the back bedroom.

"Wait a second," Jim says, freeing himself from Ed's grip. "Something's not right. I can feel it." He smiles at himself, at the sound of what he just said. "That's right, I can feel it!"

"You're damn straight things aren't right!" Ed again tries to pull Jim to the bedroom. "We need to get you on board."

But Jim fights his way into the living room and plucks the VHS out of the hands of one of the prostrate Vegans.

"Something's happening to our troupe, and I think it has to do with the new guy." He goes to put the VHS in the player, but Ed storms over, rips the tape from his hand and smashes it in two on the coffee table.

"Goddamn it, I've got a show to put on, and you want me to watch movies."

Definitely not Ed. Jim can feel it in his gut. It's the Thing all right. It's got Ed, or become him, or whatever it does. But like a bad actor, it's overplaying him.

Ed dumps the VHS pieces in the kitchen trash, then smoothes out his shirt and approaches Jim with a smile. "Can I talk with you alone for a minute. One minute, I promise. Then I'll let you go." He grabs Jim by the arm once again.

"Let go of me," Jim says. "I don't know who you are." He yanks Ed's hand from his arm and twists, but Ed doesn't cry out as he expects him to do. Instead, he looks him straight in the eye and nods his head. The game is on. Jim shoves Ed backward into the Vegans and runs out the door.

He's relieved there's no sign of John's car in front of Nikki's apartment. Maybe he's in time. She answers the door and for a moment her face beams before she tries to slam the door in his face. He sticks his foot in the way.

"Ouch!" he screams through the crack in the door.

"Stop it!" Nikki yells back. "Don't pretend you can feel anything."

"But that's just it," he says. "I can feel." He reaches through the crack in the door, searching for Nikki's hand, but she pulls it away. "Please," he continues. "Let me in." She steps away from the door, and Jim steps inside, only to find her backed against the entrance to her kitchen, arms folded, studying him.

"What are you doing here?" she asks. "Why did you come?"

"Because I love you," he says. No hesitation. No stammering.

She is caught off guard. Her eyes open. Her arms loosen. "You don't know how to love," she replies at last.

"Do you see this?" he asks, pointing to the layer of ash dusting his clothes. "That's how much I love you."

"What?" She looks about the room, stalling.

"I burned myself to cinders every night and tried to grow a new me all because I want to be with you. Because I love being with you. Because when I'm not with you I can't get you out of my head." He steps toward her, but she backs into the kitchen.

"What are you talking about?"

"I'm saying that I talk to you all day whether I'm with you or not," he says, following her into the kitchen. "You were the last thought in my head before I lit myself on fire each night, and you were the first thought in my head each morning when my new self stepped free of the garden."

She lowers her arms. "I don't believe you," she says. "Why couldn't you love me when we were going out?"

He tries to take her hand, but again she pulls it away. "I was afraid."

"You? Afraid?" She shakes her head. "You're the great Thing. The terrible monster. I don't buy it."

"I was lonely," he says, simply.

"What?"

"Lonely," he says again, almost softer than before. "I couldn't name it until today. A deep loneliness that held my feelings in its fist." He reaches for her, and she backs into the wall, putting her arms in front of her to stop him. He takes her head in his hands and kisses her. She slaps him, hard.

"How dare you!" she says. How dare you come in here pretending to be someone else, someone I might love."

"I'm not the one pretending," he says, taking her in his arms, kissing her face, her neck. "I love you. I've always loved you. I just didn't know how to let it out."

"I don't believe you." She hits him in the chest. Once. Twice. Then, rapidly as she screams. "Get out of here! Get out!"

He takes her by the wrists and pins her arms against the wall. He moves his body into her, pressing against her as he kisses her. She fights him at first, but then opens her mouth to him. Soon, he is peeling away her blouse and kissing her breasts. A minute later he is working his hand under her skirt, all the while holding her to the wall with his other hand.

"You excite me, Jim," she whispers. "Your passion excites me."

That's all he needs to hear, and he takes her right there against the wall. When it's over, they lie side by side on the kitchen floor barely able to breathe.

"That was the best sex I've ever had," she says. "I didn't know I could feel so much."

"It was pretty amazing, wasn't it?" he says, smiling. He takes her hand in his, caresses it.

"You have so much passion inside you," she continues. "Where did it come from?" She rolls over on him, looks into his eyes. Her hand reaches down between his legs, massaging him.

"It's always been there, waiting for you, for this moment. I just didn't know how to let it out." He is happy now. He can feel it. Nothing is forced. Nothing hidden. Only the two of them together, inhabiting the same space, breathing each other's breath.

"I want more of this moment," she replies, kissing her way down his body. "Lots more."

He smiles, giving himself to the pleasure, as she takes him in her mouth. But then it strikes him. She used to hate blowjobs. She'd complain about getting pubic hair in her teeth. He watches her. She seems to like it now. She's getting into it in fact, moving her head about like crazy. "Are you sure you want to do this?" he asks. "Hmm" is all she answers. She's never wanted more before, either. In fact, he often wondered if she were frigid because she'd just lie there the one time they would do it. Of course, that had been fine for him, too. Sex for them used to be mechanical. Maybe she's just excited by his passion. Maybe it stirred something in her as well. Yes, that's it. "I love you, Nikki," he says, but she again only answers "Hmm." She's really getting into this, he thinks. That's good, right? That's what he wants. Still, it bothers him. It's not the Nikki he's used to. Besides, he wants intimacy. Real intimacy. He wants to know the person he loves.

He sits up and stops her. "No, Nikki, I mean I really love you."

She looks at him strangely and smiles. "I love you, too," she says. "But right now I want you." She tries to push him back down and take him in her mouth.

He rolls her off him, but she tries to wrestle him, kissing him on the mouth, the neck as he'd done earlier.

"This is fun," she says.

"Stop it!" he cries, standing up, pushing her off him. "I don't know who you are."

She picks up her clothes and covers herself with them. "What the hell are you talking about?"

"Who are you?"

"I'm Nikki," she says. "The girl you said you loved five minutes ago." She starts putting her clothes back on, clearly irritated.

"But what if you're not?" he asks, studying her. The same dark eyes. The same full lips. The same beautiful neckline.

"If I'm not, it's because you're different." She turns away from him. "You changed me with your passion. God, I've never felt anything like it." She begins to cry.

He moves to her, ready to console her, but then suddenly feels afraid. "You could be John."

"What are you talking about?"

"How would I really know?" he asks himself. "I mean, he could have gotten to everyone by now. And then I fall in love with you, but you're not you. You're him!"

She turns on him now, eyebrows arched and mouth set in anger. "I knew you had a fear of intimacy. You son-of-a-bitch! I knew it all along. And now you come back here and win me over, just to break my heart again!"

"You don't understand," he says, reaching out to take her hand, but then hesitating, pocketing his hands. "I think he's already taken over Ed and Dewey and Paul. How do you know who to trust?"

Go!" she screams. "Get out!" She runs at him, pushing him toward the door, but he is heading there anyway.

He's got to get to the bottom of this. If he's going to feel, he's got to know who it's safe to feel with.

This time, he enters his house through the front door. The shantytown is gone, and for a moment, he thinks the Vegans are, too, until he sees the altar set up around the fireplace. Movie stills from *The Thing from Another World* line the mantle. Strings of carrots hang in front of the fireplace, and carrots cover the floor. Inside the fireplace, they've constructed a life-size model of him made out of potato sacks, arms outstretched awaiting the flame. It looks as if someone has also painted a fresco around the fireplace depicting his crash landing on earth all those years ago, his thawing out and subsequent rampage, etc. He doesn't have time to look at the details. Instead, he heads straight for the kitchen junk drawer where he pulls out a lighter and a wire from an old lamp he'd always meant to repair. Last of all, he goes to the bathroom for the scissors with which he used to cut off his own fingers. Only when he's leaving back through the kitchen does he notice the Vegans performing some sort of ceremony out in his garden. The leader is holding up a handful of dirt and sprinkling it over the heads of his followers. He opens the window to tell them to clear out.

"I baptize you with ash in the name of the Thing from Another World. May you be reborn in his image. A superior vegetable who will lead humanity to that distant world on the day of reckoning."

"Hey!" he shouts. "You all really need to go home now." When they hear his voice, they fall prostrate and begin rolling about the ground, shaking, and speaking in tongues. "Oh brother," he says and closes the window.

Everyone is already gathered in the rehearsal room

when Jim arrives. Paul, Ken, and Dewey sit squished together on the couch talking about what shows they'd like to do next season, if there is a next season. Nikki and John stand beside the couch, John's arm wrapped about Nikki's waist. Ed stands before them all, preparing to make a speech, Doug beside him sipping his coffee and nodding his agreement as Ed goes over what he wants to say.

"Listen, people," Ed begins. "We've got a show to do and precious little time to get it ready."

They nod in agreement, especially Paul, Ken, and Dewey. Jim doesn't hear a thing. All he can do is look at the way John's hand holds Nikki at the waist. He's not going to lose her again. No way.

"I don't need to tell you how much work lies ahead for us," Ed continues. "We'll have to move to a two-a-day rehearsal schedule."

Paul, Ken, and Dewey nod at the same time, as if they were one organism. Jim's sure of it. What about John? He's too cool a customer to give himself away. And Nikki? He can't tell.

"Things will be different now," Ed says, his voice moving into Henry the Fifth mode as he prepares to give a rousing speech. "I can see it in your eyes. You're coming here with a different attitude. We're a real acting troupe now, and it's time we showed the world what we can do."

Paul, Ken, and Dewey shout their agreement in unison. Doug nods his head vigorously. Nikki claps her hands, but Jim can't decide how much she's buying into Ed's speech. John seems to be observing everything.

"These next two weeks will separate the men from the boys," Ed goes on. "The women from..."

"That's exactly what I propose," Jim says, stepping between Ed and the other actors, holding his scissors aloft. "Some of us are not what we seem."

"What the hell are you doing?" Ed says.

"You are not the same actors I used to call friends," Jim continues. "Something has happened to this troupe since John joined, and I say it's time we find out what it is."

"Are you crazy?" Doug says.

"That's it, you're fired," Ed says. "We'll find a new Wall. We'll use a chair or something. I don't care. Just get out of here!"

Jim looks about him, gauging the faces of the others. Paul, Ken, and Dewey seem frightened. John is still cool and collected. Nikki brings her hands to her face, as if she's praying. Is she worried for him? Or worried she'll be embarrassed by him?

"I'd like you all to submit to a blood test," Jim says. "I'm going to make a small cut in your palm, then collect the blood."

"You've got to be out of your mind," Ed says.

"Doug, give me your coffee cup," Jim goes on. "I need something to collect the blood."

Doug holds his coffee close to his chest with both hands.

"Nobody is cutting my hand open," Paul, Ken, and Dewey shout.

But Jim has gone too far to stop now. He grabs the coffee cup from Doug and dumps the dregs on the floor.

"What exactly are you trying to do?" John says at last.

"Aren't you the smart one," Jim replies. "Standing there so cool. Pretending you don't know what's going on. Well, you're going to be first."

"First for what?" John asks. "Why don't you tell us before we call the police and have you committed."

"Some of you are not who you pretend to be," Jim goes on, taking out his wire and his lighter. "All I have to do is heat up this wire and touch it to a sample of each of your blood. If one of you is this new-fangled Thing, your blood will jump right out of this cup."

"I get it," Ed says. "You saw John's movie, and you want to re-enact the part where Kurt Russell tests to see who is real and who is the Thing?"

"Aren't you the smart one," John says.

"You really have gone over the deep end, haven't you?" Doug says.

"Jim, please..." Nikki begs.

But he can't listen to her now. He approaches John and demands that he stick out his hand.

"You don't really believe everything you see in movies, do you?" John steps away from him, appealing to the other actors. "Your friend here thinks that we are all aliens. He thinks I've infected you like some sort of virus." John turns on Jim. "Well, I've got news for the has been, walking carrot. Carpenter made up that test. He thought up the whole thing because it made for a thrilling scene. That's all movies are about. That's all we're about. Making the audience believe something that isn't real."

"It looks like some of us believed a little too well," Ed says, taking the scissors out of Jim's hand.

"When you walk out of the theatre, it's bye bye pretend," John continues, taking the lighter from Jim's other hand. "Each of us is left with the life we're dealt.

And you, my friend, are a carrot."

Nikki looks as if she is about to cry. "Come with me, Nikki," Jim says, reaching his hand out to her. "Let's start our own company. Maybe go to Indiana. I hear the community theatre scene in Fort Wayne is pretty good."

Nikki steps forward, hesitantly. She shakes her head as if unsure what to do.

"Don't listen to him, Nikki," John says, stepping between them. "Think of what we can have. No fights. No doubts. No worry about who the other is because we would know exactly who the other is. We would be free to love each other."

"Free to love yourself," Jim says. "That's nothing but masturbation." Jim steps in front of John and looks Nikki in the eye.

"I don't know who you are, Nikki, and frankly I don't care," he says. "I love you. I love the differences. The fact that you like to sleep in late, and I don't. The fact that you love to be social, and I hate people." He looks about the room. "Sorry everyone," he says, then turns back to Nikki. "I love the fact that you like the city, and I only want to garden. I even love the fact that you like pop music, and I love bluegrass." He stops and thinks better of it. "Well, maybe not that, but you see my point."

"I certainly see your point, John says, "And it sounds like a recipe for disaster."

Nikki looks from one Thing to the other.

Jim again reaches out for her hand. "Nikki, please," he says. "Trust in us." But he can't read her face. Too many things have happened. Too many changes over too short a time.

"Come on, Nikki," John says, grabbing her and

making a run for it. Jim dives for John and grabs him about the waist, tackling him. The two wrestle about on the floor.

"Great!" Ed exclaims. "That's it! The show is over. There's no hope now."

Paul, Ken, and Dewey look like they want to get up and leave but are afraid to move. Doug follows Ed about as he paces, trying to tell him things will work out. Nikki covers her face with her hands, shouting, "Stop it!"

John pins Jim, but just as he smiles in victory, Jim bites him on the hand. John rolls off and starts to shake violently.

"Do you see this?" Jim says. "This is what I'm talking about. How can you call that acting? He looks like an overgrown Mexican jumping bean." Jim looks toward Ed, saying, "You hired this guy…" when a tentacle shoots out of John's mouth and wraps around Jim's neck. Nikki screams. Paul, Ken, and Dewey look one to the other. "Oh, this is just great," Jim says, though it's difficult to breathe. He tries to turn to Nikki, but the tentacle only tightens about his neck. A few seconds later, he blacks out.

John stands and gathers himself, the tentacle disappearing back inside his mouth. "Well," he says. "The show must go on. What do you say we start those two-a-days?"

"Great idea," Ed says, setting the scissors on the end table beside the couch. "Paul. Dewey. Let's go. We'll start with the fathers."

The actors gather for the scene and begin rehearsing. Jim opens his eyes. It's a good thing vegetables are anaerobic. He could go without oxygen for much longer if he needed to. Another reason they are the superior race. He spots Nikki standing beside the others. She is crying, seeming unsure what to do. He jumps up and steps toward her just as the others sing: *Plant a radish, get a radish not a Brussels sprout. . .*

"Hey," Doug shouts. "Jim's alive!"

John starts shaking again, tentacles shooting out of his chest. One of them lassoes Jim's ankle. Just as Jim's falling to the ground, he eyes the scissors on the table. He crawls for them and reaches out even as the tentacle pulls him toward John. He tries again for the scissors and knocks the table over, the scissors falling away. Dewey runs to pick them up, but instead kicks them toward Jim. He grabs them and in one action cuts the tentacle holding his ankle. Jim jumps to his feet and holds the scissors out in front of him, waving them at the others. "Don't take another step!" he shouts. "Any of you!"

He looks at Nikki, who seems somehow closer to the others than before. He studies her face, trying to guess what she feels. But her face is a blank.

"Is it you, Nikki?" he asks.

She doesn't answer. Maybe she's too stunned to talk. Maybe she loves him but is afraid to say it. Maybe she's one of them. How can he know? How will he ever know? Fear chokes him, and for a moment he thinks John's got another tentacle around his neck. So, this is what it means to feel. To put your love out there and risk it all. Nikki's gaze shifts back and forth between him and John. Nothing is certain, Jim thinks. Except loneliness.

He reaches out and grabs Nikki before she can react. She looks at him, shakes her head no. She starts to pull her hand away. He grips her hand tighter. "I'm not letting you go," he whispers. She nods her head, and they both back slowly toward the door. Once he's in the hallway, he hears Ed shout, "Get him!" Jim slams the door closed and nearly bumps into the janitor who is mopping the floor and whistling, "Try to Remember." Jim grabs the mop from him and jams it through the door handle just as the other actors pound into the door. He thanks the janitor, then grabs Nikki's hand. He tries to read her, but she looks so scared. "Is this what you want?" he asks. *Yes,* her eyes seem to say. *Maybe.* The two run down the hall and out into an afternoon thunderstorm.

They are immediately soaked. But they don't care. They hold each other, spinning around in the rain. "We did it!" Jim exclaims, kissing her. "We did it! Now we can be together." He looks to the sky, but the dark clouds appear heavy with hail. "We better get out of here," he says. They climb into his car and kiss even as the hail pings on the roof and windshield. He holds her hand as they drive down the road, exiting onto I-70. "Let's head east," he says, smiling at her. She smiles back, tentatively. "It will be okay," he tells her, though his mouth is so dry the words almost don't make it out. "We'll be okay." He squeezes her hand, and she squeezes back. A bit stronger than usual, he thinks. She's just scared. Like I am. It doesn't mean anything. We know who we are. He looks ahead and hopes they'll be able to outrace the storm.

Photo by Gary Isaacs

PETER GRANDBOIS is the author of the novel *The Gravedigger*, selected by Barnes and Noble for its "Discover Great New Writers" program, *The Arsenic Lobster: A Hybrid Memoir*, chosen as one of the top five memoirs of 2009 by the Sacramento News and Review, *Nahoonkara*, winner of the gold medal in literary fiction in *ForeWord* magazine's Book of the Year Awards for 2011, and a collection of surreal flash fictions, *Domestic Disturbances*. His essays, plays, and short stories have appeared in numerous journals and been shortlisted for both the Pushcart Prize and Best American Essays. He is an associate editor at *Boulevard* magazine and teaches at Denison University in Ohio.

CPSIA information can be obtained at www.ICGtesting.com
Printed in the USA
LVOW11s1048280914

406234LV00007B/756/P